Boardwalk, Blackmail

and Beach *Music*

A Nikki Rodriguez Mystery

M.A. Hansen

Cover art is designed by Mariah Sinclair, mariahsinclair.com

Prologue

The summer sun shone bright over the crowd of people standing with solidarity at the sight of the grand dam herself, the Rancho Santa Arianna Mansion and Estate. Currently, the estate is held as a museum with lush gardens and lake views.

Roxy Carmichael, president of The Arts and Preservation Society, spoke clearly and concisely at the podium in front of the boat dock by the lake.

"We must preserve this estate for the future of our community. We owe it to past generations to continue to carry on in support of our historical buildings." Nikki sat in a chair to the left of the podium, quietly listening to Roxy's speech.

The large crowd had doubled in size this afternoon since word of the protest had circulated the city, many came from other cities as well to show support for the historical preservation society - Rancho Niguel chapter, which partnered up with The Arts and Preservation Society.

"We must stop the vicious greed perpetrating our communities to demolish our founding homes and lands that built our communities. Don't we have enough condos? Don't we have enough mini-malls? The historical society and I have come up with

some wonderful options to bring in funding for the upkeep of the estate built in 1903.

We have put our ideas together and have come up with turning this 20-acre estate into a non-profit fabulous lodge or Inn, with room for events and galas, a fine art museum, a spa, and 50 guest rooms for affordable vacation rental fees all year long overlooking the lake. As for this boat launch, we look forward to turning it into a full-time marina, renting out boat slips for moorage, and keeping prices at record-low levels for all of the community to afford. The current boathouse will also rent out boats, canoes, kayaks, and windboards. On the grounds, we will also add some small cottages lakefront for vacation rental. Plus, maintenance on the pool.

The cost has come to $5 million dollars to upgrade and renovate the estate, with a grant obtained by the county for more than half of that amount. We have private donations that have come in for 1.5 million dollars, so now we have to raise $500,000 dollars. All of the funds from the inn and boat rentals will go to provide estate upkeep and staff payroll, security services, and a public park. So what do you say, ladies and gentlemen, we can do it!"

Later that night, when everyone had left the lake for the evening, a man drove up to the mansion and parked his Porsche in the circular driveway. He opened his car door and walked to the front of the mansion entryway. A grand entrance with a lush green lawn and a vast garden, the man stood to the side of the huge concrete fountain with a mural of mermaids engraved in green stone. The fountain sat low, but in front of the estate, it made for an elegant entrance. Soon, another lone figure walked toward the man, the figure handed the man an envelope the size of a letter.

"Here is the report on the stability of this dump. It needs about $5 million in renovations, and they don't have the money to cover it. The city wants it sold and fast before the protesters are really heard."

The man looked over the contents of the envelope!

"So it's a done deal, I can purchase the estate and then demolish it for my 300-plus condo community?"

"Sure, but we have to get it through the city council vote. The Mayor will do whatever they say."

"That's no problem, I have secured three members who will vote my way."

The man smiled despite his nefarious business dealings.

"Whatever, do you have my money?" The stranger asked.

"Here."

The man handed off a white handle bag filled with $100s in four stacks.

The stranger took out a counterfeit pen, "It's not that I don't trust you but I don't trust you."

"It's real and all there." The man said, sarcasm dripping from his words.

The stranger finished up and put the money back in the bag.

"Ok, I'll be in touch."

The man got back in his Porsche, and the stranger walked off.

The man turned on his car and drove away laughing to himself,

"By next week, I'll have made myself richer than I ever imagined."

Chapter 1

Boats, Boats, Boats

The grand opening this morning was spectacular. Little Black Dress, among three other bands, performed on the new boardwalk on Lake Santa Arianna. We kicked off to the tune of "Soak Up the Sun" By Sheryl Crow.

With the lake under us, shimmering in the sunshine, boats drifted in the distance, and people made their way strolling the boardwalk to the end of the pier where we had the stage. Snack stands and retail booths were in full motion, servicing many customers. Kids with their parents strolled with balloons in yellow, white, and emerald green, holding large swirls of pink cotton candy.

The smell of hot dogs grilled and burgers sizzling wafted through the air. My stomach growled just from the thought of food at this time. Breakfast this morning had been skimpy, just coffee and a bagel with cream cheese, and now I was more than ready for lunch. The band played two more songs, "Is This Love" by Bob Marley and "Hot Fun in the Summertime" By Sly and The Family Stone. This song makes you just want to take a stroll on the boardwalk. I sang the song as a duet with Tito, with the girls playing the

7

background music and vocals. We wrapped it up to a cheering audience. After stepping down from the stage, the band met up at The Burger Shack.

We sat down at a table on the patio. Cheeseburgers all around and iced teas.

"I love singing with you gals."

Tito said, taking a drink of his Iced tea.

"We've been doing some great duet songs. Why didn't we think of this before?" I replied.

"Hey, Tito, did you bring your boat?" Roxy asked.

"I sure did, Daisy and I dropped it off in a slip an hour and a half ago, she's meeting me back here in about 20 minutes. She had to go and get some snacks and drinks. You guys all up for skirting around the lake?" He asked us.

"Not for us Tito, we have a baseball game with our company." Dana and Taylor, my band members replied.

"I've got a baby shower for my sister-in-law later today guys, rain check?" Emily, my other guitarist, asked.

"Sure, we have all summer, it's only early August, this is California, we can boat well into November." Tito smiled, his pearly whites gleaming."

"August 1, to be exact, so that means we have like 90 days or something, right?" Roxy asked.

The new band on stage began with "Don't Worry Baby."

By The Beach Boys.

We sang along to the song briefly, "I love this song." I said out loud to everyone.

"Ladies and Tito, congratulations on a fabulous job. I caught the show here." Matt came up behind our table, walking into the patio dressed in a pair of blue Hawaiian print board shorts, a light grey t-shirt, and slip-on white Vans.

"Thanks," I replied.

"Have a seat." Roxy told Matt.

He sat down across from me next to Tito; he looked like he had been out on the lake already, his tan a shade darker.

"So what's new Matt?" Roxy asked him.

"I bought a new boat." He smiled.

"What, no way, the Bayliner you were looking at, congrats man!" Tito bro'd a high five with Matt.

"Yeah, I just got the keys a few days ago. I have her in the lake at the boat house right now. You guys want to go for a ride?"

I shot a look at Tito. I was going out with Daisy and him in a few minutes, but before I spoke up, Roxy intercepted.

9

"Matt, I promised I would go out with Tito and Daisy, but Nikki can go with you."

Tito piped in, "Yeah, Nikki, we'll catch you later."

Matt smiled and turned to me, "How about it?"

I had been blindsided by my bestie, and now Tito! Once again, Cupid's apprentice, Roxy the heart maker, set me up. I thought of calling her Madam Roxy, maybe that was more fitting for her. I didn't have time to shoot her a look of "Oh no, lady, stop setting me up," but it was too late. Matt was staring at me with those amazing baby blues, patiently waiting for an answer.

"Yeah, that sounds like fun. I just need to change." I pointed to my boat tote bag in red and beige canvas.

"The boathouse has a changing cabana." Matt offered.

I had no way out of this one, so I agreed with a smile. "Sure, that would be fine."

We all got up from the table and made our way out. I said bye to the gals in my band and, away from Matt's eyes, I shot Roxy a look that said we'll talk later, girlfriend!

She laughed and said, "Have fun, you two!"

Tito just smiled and gave me the thumbs-up signal.

I had changed in the boat house cabana, a small room with a bathroom and a mirrored vanity.

Today I sported a tankini bathing suit, it's so cute, the color is a beautiful, vibrant dark blue and white in a hibiscus floral print. A halter spaghetti strap, and the bottoms are the same color and pattern. I saw it last week while shopping in Laguna Beach and grabbed one. I added a white long-sleeve seersucker button-down shirt over my suit.

I put my clothes in my bag and put on my white slip-on Keds; better to have anti-slip footing on a boat, right?

I walked down to the slip where Matt's boat sat slowly moving with the current of the lake. Anchored at this time and steady enough for me to ease on into the back of the boat, Matt held my hand to help me in.

It was very nice, the outside of the boat was two-tone white on the top and dark blue on the lower part. The seats were white too, with dark blue trim.

DX2250 is what it said in small stainless steel lettering under the large cursive writing that read *Bayliner* on the side of the boat.

The boat was spotless and new, and everything was shiny and polished. The seats had the words BAYLINER on the top part of the seating area on the back of the boat. A small walkway led to the area where you could jump off the boat into the water. Along with a sunbathing deck off the back of the boat.

11

The Bow had more seating, resembling a circular seating area past the driver and passenger seats. It was like a sunk-in nook. Very cool!

I stowed my bag in a compartment under one of the bench seats and put my cell in a compartment by the steering wheel that Matt told me was waterproof.

"Find a seat and we'll head out."

He had on a pair of dark Oakley sunglasses. I selected the seat across from his and put on my shades; we were twinning. I had put my hair in a low ponytail to keep it from flying all over the place. One thing about these boats, they were hell on hair.

He started the engine, and off we went, gliding into the blue water in the blazing sun.

We sped around the large lake a few times, going by other boats and passing the large Rancho Santa Arianna Mansion and Estate. Matt turned on the speakers and put music on, via Bluetooth on his phone. After a few hours, we pulled into a nice little spot on the other side of the lake with views of the hills. He turned off the engine, and we anchored for a snack. He pulled out some drinks from a small fridge under the small sink in the middle of the boat. He handed me a Coke and asked me to put the small portable table on the back seats. I went ahead and placed it in the holes on the bottom of the seats, and we had a table for our lunch. The song "Boat Ride" By Brian Kelley played on the speakers. Matt brought out two plastic blue plates with cold fried chicken, potato salad, and a bowl of cold strawberries. His boat had a retractable canopy above, giving us some much-needed shade!

"You did good, Captain Stevens, this is exactly what I wanted for lunch."

He smiled back at me and then took a bite of his chicken, I know it's one of your favorites."

"Yours too, buddy, and the country music, this is totally you!" I chuckled.

"Don't knock the country, you know I'm just a cowboy at heart."
He laughed, touching his heart to show his love for being a cowboy.

We had some small talk about current events in the city and his team at the firehouse, the band, Kendle's, and my new Jeep. The music went from "Summer Time" to "Guitars and Tiki Bars" by Kenny Chesney.

"So tell me the truth, how are you really?"

I knew he was wondering if I was still upset about Nick Williams dumping me at Sara's party last month. I was over him, truthfully, but I felt like being dumped was becoming normal for me.

"I'm over it all, really. It's a good thing he left; he was more committed to his career, and I don't think it would have worked in the long run anyway."

"I didn't see you as a doctor's wife, honestly." Matt replied.

"Whoa, who said anything about marriage?" I commented in a slow-down, dude kind of attitude.

"I know it scares you." He carefully stated.

I wasn't sure what he meant by that comment; should I be offended or complimented?

"I'm going to be honest, someday, yes, of course I'd like to get married and have kids, the house, and the family pets, but I'm doing it on my terms."

"I wouldn't expect anything less. You are very independent, and that scares some guys."

"Does that include you too?"

"I'll be honest, no! Nick was a fool! He didn't understand who you were and what he had!

I admit I had been a fool too! I was upset about the whole Sara issue, and it took me four months to see why you did what you did, and even though I don't agree with you keeping it from me, I understand why you did."

"So you're still not over it?" I asked with a little ice in my voice.

"I'm over it! I realized that if you had to lie to me to protect someone in my family whom I love very much, then that sacrifice is honorable. I'm not going to be a fool again, Nikki Rodriguez. I want you back."

Chapter 2

Under The Boardwalk, Oh No!

After our meal, we took the boat around one more time, gliding through the blue water of the lake and relaxing to the tunes of beachy/ island music. "Margarita Ville" by Jimmy Buffett played, and then "Stir It Up" by Bob Marley. We swam in cool blue water for a while like young teenagers, laughing and joking around with one another. Really talking and listening to one another. I also had a chance to sunbathe on that lovely deck. I thought about what Matt said; he wanted to get back together.

I told him it was a little soon from my last relationship, but that we should be friends and continue to let it naturally evolve. I also told him I still had feelings for Paul, and until that was resolved, I wasn't making any relationship official.

He agreed and told me that was fair and that he wanted our relationship built on trust and full commitment. Yeah, that word was scary, but he didn't push, and we decided to just move along slowly. After one more go around the lake, we decided to call it a day.

I was glad that I had put on sunblock, and now my tan became more Hawaiian tropical island girl.

It was around 5:30 pm, and even though the lake was still filled with boaters and jet skiers, and the sun was still high, but we were tired.

I opened my beach bag, pulled on a pair of denim shorts, and tied my shirt at the waist. Matt docked the boat in one of the boat slips, and we made our way towards the boardwalk. Matt volunteered to drive me home since I didn't have my car here. I told him I had to make one stop first. I had to go to the city sub-office located at the end of the boardwalk by the restaurant called The Lake House.

"I'll just be a minute. I need to pick up the check for the band from Emma, the city office manager."

"Ok, I'll wait here." Matt stood outside the small office building hub, leaning on a lamp post, checking his phone. I walked into the small office and spotted Emma.

She was getting ready to lock up, her pale pink summer dress still looked fabulous, the crisp linen without a wrinkle. "Nikki, I'm so glad you're here. I was going to just mail your check off, but now that you're here, well, here you go."

She handed me a white envelope with the city logo, a mountain in blue with the sun in yellow, setting down. I had come to know these envelopes very well, having a city check cut for the band over the last six years or so.

"Thank you, Emma, if you have any other events you need us for, just give me a ring." I told her heading for the door.

"Nikki, I did want to ask you a question."

"What is it, Emma?" I asked, wondering what this was about.

"I was wondering, are you still friends with Detective Anderson?"

This caught me a little off guard. Why would Emma want to know this? I had only interacted with her professionally as a city employee, never discussing anything private or for a social conversation.

"Yes, we are friends still." I smiled politely.

"I know this may sound strange since we are business acquaintances, but I'm worried about Detective Anderson."

"Why? What's going on?"

"It has to do with Stacie."

I was intrigued with my ears on full-blown high-frequency.

"Please go on." I said.

"Marge and I are good friends, and we were talking about Stacie one day, and we came to the conclusion that she has some ulterior motives for her job and for Detective Anderson.

18

So Marge confided in me about what she thinks Stacie is after, and so I've been watching her as well, and yesterday I noticed that she and the mayor went to her house, and they didn't return for several hours. Then, when Mayor CJ returned, she looked like a ghost; her eyes were clear, but it was like she wasn't in the moment; she looked like she was in a trance or something. When I tried to speak with her, Stacie cut between us and said that Mayor CJ was suffering from a migraine and she had taken some medication. I told Marge it was so strange, it didn't seem like Mayor CJ knew what was happening to her."

"What kind of medication did she take?"

"Stacie said it was aspirin." Emma said, looking like it was a strange thing.

"Aspirin wouldn't have that kind of reaction for her." I responded.

"Nikki, then when she went to lunch with Detective Anderson on another day, he had that same look on his face, and Stacie said he was just tired from solving the case last week about the murder of Kristin Cabela and saving Nikki's Hyde once again. She said it in a very menacing way, too!"

"Emma, let me look into this and I'll be in touch, ok."

"Thanks, Nikki, I just feel like there's something not right." Her look of concern had caused me worry and intrigue. What was Stacie up to this time?

I walked out of the office, and Matt and I walked slowly, as of course, my mind was spinning with questions and thoughts. I reached into my bag, took out my cashmere wrap, and draped it around my shoulders, and the chill in the air suddenly came on. We reached the end of the pier/boardwalk, and Matt broke the silence. "I was wondering if you were still here; you seemed distracted."

"Oh, sorry, it's nothing, I'm just tired, a little too much sun, I guess." I said nonchalantly, dismissing it.

I walked on and went down the side ramp from the pier to the edge of the lake. Matt followed me. I stood on the sand, looking at the blue, calm water, thinking about what Emma told me.

"Nikki, are you ready to go?" Matt asked as he stood beside me. Just then, the wind picked up, and my wrap, which I had around my shoulders, went flying away. Matt and I chased it as it headed under the pier.

"That's my favorite wrap, it's silk and cashmere." I said, running to get it. Matt was just a little bit ahead of me and stopped for an instant.

"Nikki, I think you might need to replace it."

 When I caught up to him, my white wrap lay on top of a body in

the bloody sand under the boardwalk!

"Oh no!"

I said out loud!

Chapter 3

Murder On The Beach

Paul and Craig were the detectives on the scene this evening. Sonya, another police detective and my friend, was on vacation in Mexico with her husband, so it was just the boys on the case. Craig was interviewing Matt, and Paul came over to speak with me.

"Nikki, are you ok?" He put his hand on my shoulder.

"Just a little shaken right now." I replied.

"Take a deep breath, let it go, and just take your time. Just start from the beginning and tell me what happened?" His green eyes filled with concern. My ruined cashmere wrap, now a dark burgundy from the blood it soaked up, was in a plastic evidence bag with one of the CS investigators.

I gave Paul the rundown from the time Matt and I left the city hub office on the boardwalk, to the wind coming and taking my wrap, and when we followed to retrieve it, to the point where we found him! He wrote down every detail, not missing a beat.

"Ok, it looks like I have all of the information I need right now. I'll give you a call if I need anything else." Paul said, closing his small notebook and walking away to get one last detail from the coroner. I thought about the body lying there in the sand under the boardwalk. How long had he been there? The coroner had packed up the body and driven the van off to the morgue to do the autopsy. I went over the whole thing again in my mind, making sure I gave every detail to Paul I could possibly remember. A few minutes later, I walked over to Craig, and Matt to chat, and then Paul joined us a few minutes later.

"Any idea who this guy was? How long has he been dead?" I asked.

"He's been dead about two hours, and the body belongs to Hawkins McGuire, better known as the Hawk, real estate tycoon." Craig responded.

"The man who wants to tear down the Rancho Santa Arianna Mansion! Oh my gosh!" I raked my hand through my hair in disbelief.

"Bingo!" Craig replied, punctuating this with his finger in the air.

"No way!" Matt called out, astonished, rubbing his jaw.

"Yeah, the big mogul that has been havoc on SoCal."
Paul chimed in.

The reputation of Hawk, the real estate mogul, was that he tore down old historical homes and buildings and made way for shiny and new commercial or residential buildings, all crammed together with minimal architecture and cheap materials.

"Who would kill him, though?" I asked. Paul and Craig looked at one another.

"We do have a possible suspect." Paul said quietly.

"Who?" Matt and I asked in unison.

"Roxy." Paul said with a look of concern.

"What! How or why?" I asked in disbelief.

"The murder weapon was found under the body; he was stabbed with a drumstick!" Craig told us.

"That's ridiculous, Roxy would never. She would never hurt anyone, let alone use one of her drumsticks. I don't believe it!" I clamored.

"Roxy wouldn't do this." Matt called out, shaking his head no!

"We have to follow the evidence, Nikki. I don't make the rules." Paul responded with a glare.

He walked off to talk to a fellow officer in blues.

"I gotta get going, Nikki, I don't think Roxy did it either." Craig said, then he headed off to the other officers clustered around the crime scene.

24

"You ready to go home, Nikki?"

"Yes."

I walked to Matt's red truck in a daze, replaying the conversation that had just taken place. Matt drove to the boat launch and retrieved his boat, hooked it up to the trailer hitch on the back of his truck, and locked it in place.

I got in the truck and we drove off. Soft music played from his XM radio, "Little Surfer Girl" by The Beach Boys.

When we got to my place, I thanked Matt for a cool day on the lake, but I had to talk to Roxy and fast.

He understood and told me if I needed anything to call him and tell Roxy that he's on her side.

"Thanks, Matt, see ya later." I grabbed my bag and went into my condo. I dialed Roxy's number and told her what happened.

"Roxy, I'm calling my stepdad, Jeff's lawyer. Don't say a word to Paul or Craig, just tell them you will need to speak with legal counsel."

"Well, Nikki, you might want to hurry; they just showed up."

"Don't say a word!"

"Ok."

Chapter 4

Attorney Please

After I hung up with Roxy, I dialed the family attorneys at the Wexler, Hyatt, Newman, and Johnson firm.

The office said they would send their top criminal attorney out right away, so I gave them Roxy's address.

I quickly changed into a pair of black pants and a black and white silk sleeveless blouse. I put on some black low-heeled sandals, grabbed my keys, and drove over to Roxy's place.

Paul and Craig's police car, Charger, was parked outside of Roxy's apartment. She lived in a four-plex off of Main Street, next to the movie theatre.

I knocked on the door, and Roxy let me in. I hugged her and went in. Roxy's platinum blonde do was set in a low bun with her usual red chopsticks crosswise in her hair. She was dressed in an A-line sleeveless dress in a dark floral print.

Paul and Craig were having a glass of water at the kitchen table.

"Did you say anything?" I whispered to Roxy.

"No, they just got here."

I walked over to Detective Anderson and Detective Zane.

"Nikki, what are you doing here?"

Paul asked, not happy to see me!

"Roxy is waiting for legal counsel. The lawyer should be here soon."

Paul stood up.

"We just need to ask Roxy a few questions; it's routine, that's it."

"Then you won't mind if she has a lawyer." I replied.

I sat down and smiled.

"Craig, how is Kiana doing?"

"Great, Nikki, thanks for asking." He smiled.

Paul glared at him, Craig sat up straighter, and then began.

"Nikki, maybe we should just get this over with. We're not arresting Roxy, just questioning her."

The doorbell rang, and Roxy ran to answer it. Roxy came back with a tall gal in a dark blue suit. Her flawless makeup on her cocoa skin was smooth without a wrinkle.

"I'm Deidre Johnson, legal counsel for Ms. Carmichael!" She put her hand out to Paul and Craig.

"Detective Anderson, and this is Detective Zane, let's get started." He said point-blank, but with a brash of harshness at the end of his sentence.

"Detectives, I've been briefed on the evidence you have, and there are no fingerprints, no records of my client having any connection to the murder weapon. Plus, she has an alibi. After being on stage for two hours, she was on the boat all afternoon with friends and then went to dinner with the same group of friends, and I have witnesses willing to testify to it. This meeting is over, fellas!"

Wow, this woman kicked butt! She left Craig with his mouth open, gaping at the marvel of Miss Deidra's control of the conversation. Paul stood up, not happy with the conversation, but he knew she was right. "We have letters that were written to the victim from Roxy, and there is the motive to remove Mr. McGuire so that he wouldn't be in her way to purchase and demolish the Rancho Santa Arianna Mansion." He told her.

"All of the letters were written in a business and professional manner, with CC copies sent to the Mayor herself. As for motive, you have no evidence of that, and all of it is speculation."

Paul and Craig made their way to the door. Craig left his business contact card with Deidra, and they walked out to their car.

After Craig and Paul left, Deidra sat down and went over what they had.

"Ladies, they have nothing, and I am aware that you had a dislike for the victim, but that is all, and if everyone who disliked someone were arrested, everyone would be in jail. If they want to speak with you, tell them you will only do so with me there."

"Wow, you were amazing, you must be the best lawyer I've ever met." Roxy told her.

"She was top of her class at Stanford, and Miss Deidra just became the youngest female to make partner at her firm. You know Jeff only hires the best." I winked.

"Oh, thank you, Nikki." Deidra smiled.

"Here is my private line if you need me in a hurry."

She handed Roxy her business card.

"Thanks," Roxy replied.

After Deidra left, Roxy and I had a glass of wine.

"So now this is put on my shoulders because I led the group against this guy's business." Roxy remarked.

"Look, you didn't do this, and I doubt anyone from the Rancho Historical Society or The Arts and Preservation Society would do anything like this."

"The thing is, we need to find out who would!"

Chapter 5

No Bullies Allowed

A few days later, when the news of the murder of Hawk McGuire, Real Estate mogul, died down a bit (no pun intended), the Historical Society and The Arts and Preservation Society at Rancho Niguel met at the grand mansion. Roxy, our president, along with our Executive Assistant, Rhonda Timbers, and I, the VP, were invited to the meeting with the city council and the mayor. Also in attendance was Dr. Neal Forbes from the Historical Society. The four of us sat in the main hall, a room that was used for parties and large dinners, now it was used as an auditorium for the museum. White wooden chairs sat in rows of six facing the front wall of the room.

Large windows adorned the opposite side of the room, allowing for plenty of sunlight that brought warmth. We arrived early and took our seats in the second row. A podium was placed on a six-foot table up front with chairs for the members of the city council, four of them to be exact, they were Roger Penny, Pamela Jayapal, Rose Metcalf, Jet Montrose, and, of course, Mayor CJ Groves.

"The council is set to vote today on the future of the estate, but do you think they will postpone it due to the recent events, in regard to Mr. McGuire?"

Dr. Neal Forbes asked us making conversation while we waited.

"I was told that there would be a vote today." Roxy replied.

The members of the board arrived along with the Mayor and a few representatives from Hawk McGuire's real estate firm.

"They must have carpooled together." I whispered to Roxy.

"I would be surprised they could all fit into one car with the egos in that group." We chuckled.

The mayor sat down in her seat up front by the podium, her evil Gidget hair flip now in light caramel, went lovely with her yellow floral top and white slacks. She was a stylish and smart dresser, I'd give her that.

Stacie sat down behind our row, but at the end of it, so she was four seats away from us. She had a large notebook with her and wore a low-cut lavender blouse with navy slacks and a smug look on her face. Roxy and I looked at one another, wondering what was next.

"We would like to bring this meeting to order now!"

The mayor sounded off.

The four of us sat up, poised and prepared for the vote to come.

"I would like to thank everyone for coming today despite the tragedy that has taken place right under our great new boardwalk. What a terrible thing to happen."

She looked down, now playing up the humanitarian concern.

Yeah right!

"I have spoken with the board and we have decided..."

She stopped for just a second as Craig and Paul took a seat in our row on the last two seats. I looked at Paul and smiled. He smiled back but then looked forward.

The mayor continued her speech for us. " We have decided to postpone the vote!"

"What? That's not fair!" Roxy yelled out.

I shook my head at her, telling her not to say another word!

Craig and Paul looked at Roxy. I stood up right away and said:

"Thank you, Ms. Mayor. We understand that at this time, that would be the best thing to do."

She acknowledged me with, "Nikki, I knew you would understand, and folks, we will still take your ideas and let you be heard up front at the podium. We are a civilized republic, you know."

She gave a look of intent to her words.

 "Dr. Neal Forbes, you are up first."

Evil Gidget smiled and then sat down.

I had a chance to scan the room, and it seemed we had more people from the community here now, a few of them held signs that read: SAVE RANCHO SANTA ARIANNA in red writing on white poster boards.

Dr. Forbes went to the podium and began his speech for the pro-save-the-estate side of the vote.

We clapped for him, and the protesters cheered him on. Roxy sulked in her chair, arms crossed over her chest, and her full red lips in a pout!

I had to keep her from incriminating herself, especially with Paul and Craig sitting a few seats from us.

Stacie got up from her seat and tried to squeeze into the empty seat where Dr. Forbes was sitting between Paul and Rhonda. I was next to Rhonda on her left, and of course, Dr. Forbes would be back after his speech. Who the heck did she think she was?

Rhonda had her purse sitting on the empty seat when Stacie told her:

"Can you move your purse?" She whispered, but stood with her foot tapping. I knew she just wanted to sit next to Paul.

I could see the look on Craig's face; he just raised his eyebrows. No doubt he was aware of Stacy's methods.

Rhonda, the sweet gal she was, and a little reluctant, replied, "Dr. Forbes will be coming back to his seat."

Stacie grew impatient and pushed Rhonda's purse to the floor. She sat down right away, with a look of satisfaction on her face.

Paul whispered to her, "Was that necessary? You're being rude."

Poor Rhonda just picked up her purse, but had a look of being slapped, her face was flushed pink and red. At that point, something inside me erupted!

I stood up and yelled, "You owe her an apology, Stacie!"

Dr. Forbes stopped his speech, and the room went silent!

"Oh yeah, who's going to make me?" She stood up with her hands on her hips.

Rhonda slid over to my seat, and I was face-to-face with Stacie.

"I am!" I told her, our eyes locked on one another. Craig and Paul got up now. "Ladies, let's all sit down and be calm." Craig quietly suggested.

"Shut up Craig!" Stacie spat out!

"Someone needs to teach you some manners!" I told her.

Paul's arm was on her pulling her back.

"Back off, Paul, I can handle this!" Stacie smirked, and when her open hand made contact with my face, I returned with a fist. She fell back into Paul and touched her cheek,

"My face!" She cried out!

Paul pulled her out of the aisle, and they walked off. Craig grabbed me and walked me out of the room. The commotion now had an audience that was focused on us. Dr. Forbes was still silent, and the peaceful protesters didn't utter a word, only holding up their cell phones, no doubt recording the incident.

When we got outside, Paul was lecturing Stacie on the front steps. Craig let my arm go, and then he said.

"Good left hook Nikki, that broad gets on my nerves."

Ha said drawing out the word as brawd to describe Stacie.

"She was so rude to everyone, and I guess I just blew, I'm sorry Craig. I don't believe violence is the way to go."

"You're good Nikki. She hit first, just walk it off."

I rubbed the side of my face, being slapped by someone with rings on was not cool. I could see Stacie's face swelling and some bruising coming to her cheek. Paul was really laying into her; the veins in his neck actually popped out. I had never seen him that upset. He was always so calm and cool.

A few seconds later, he walked to Craig and me. Stacie stayed planted where she was still rubbing her cheek.

"Nikki!"

"I'm sorry Paul, I shouldn't have hit her, but she hit me first."

I calmly pointed out. He didn't say anything more except.

"Are you ok?"

"I'll be fine."

By now, many people had come outside to witness the commotion. The Mayor ran over to us, "Ladies, please let's be civilized, no fighting, we can resolve our disputes peacefully, there's no reason for violence now." She said with a plastic smile.

"Everything is fine, Ms. Mayor, there is no need to worry, we have diffused the situation." Craig told her.

"Oh, good, ok, well, we adjourned the meeting, so I guess we will reconvene later next week. Stacie, I need to speak with you." The mayor called out now heading toward Stacie.

Roxy, Dr. Forbes, and Rhonda came up to me now.

"Thank you, Nikki, for standing up for me." Rhonda quietly said she had her purse on her shoulder and then calmly left for her car. Dr. Forbes shook my hand and bid Roxy and me farewell and said that he would be at the next meeting.

Roxy pulled me inside the building and we went back to the museum side of the mansion. The rooms downstairs displayed artwork, sculptures, and paintings. We went to a parlor room off the dining area, a set of two-person teak benches sat in the middle of the pale peach room.

"Nikki, I'm so glad you stood up to her. I couldn't believe how she bullied poor Rhonda."

"Roxy, I just broke. She was so mean, I just had to say something."

"Yeah, and did you see that smirk on her face when she took the seat? Man, she's really something. Then, telling Craig to shut up, you should have seen the look on his face, I thought he was going to haul her out and beat her! Does it hurt?"

She asked, scrunching her face.

"I'm good, don't worry."

We took a tour of the place, the rooms upstairs, about forty of them, reminded me of a small boutique hotel. We only saw about ten rooms, and Roxy had ideas for making each one a slight nautical theme, nothing kitschy, just more serene.

"One hundred and twenty years old, it's so classic, the built-in alcoves, bookshelves, and even the built-in buffets and hutches. You don't see 1903 architecture like this anymore, with custom crown molding and stained glass windows, lead glass chandeliers. This style is a cross between Mediterranean and turn-of-the-century style. Look at these sinks, so timeless, and all of the doorknobs are lead crystal, too. It's beautiful!" I told Roxy

"The furniture is dated circa 1901. Can you imagine destroying it? I can't." Roxy replied.

The backstory of the Rancho Santa Ariana Mansion was a romantic one, much better than fiction.

The mansion was built by Aiden Packard for his wife, Arianna Niguel. The story goes something like this: she was a wealthy socialite born to a family that owned all of Rancho Niguel or formerly the town called Haven Valley.

The family farmed citrus, oranges, limes, lemons, grapefruit, and tangerines.

They also owned the third-largest winery in the state.

Arianna, at 18, fell in love with Aiden Packard, a poor 23-year-old iron worker from Los Angeles.

The family's feeling that he didn't measure up, they forbade the reunion and sent poor Arianna away to San Francisco to attend college.

After six years of being away from home, Arianna finally came back to Haven Valley.

When she arrived, she found out that Aiden and his family had struck oil in their backyard and became the fourth-wealthiest family in the West.

Aiden went to college, earned a business degree, and became the president of Packard Oil, his family's business.

He also had a fiancée and was scheduled to be married in a few days.

Upon hearing this, Arianna went to see Aiden, and after one day together, they declared their undying love for one another and eloped the next day.

The scandal was hard for her family and they disowned her. Aiden and Arianna were happy they had three children and Aiden commissioned the home to be built on the lake in 1903 and called it Rancho Santa Arianna. Eventually, Arianna's family came around and on her father's deathbed, he left her the winery and the 1000 acres of orchards.

Aiden and Arianna happily lived at Rancho Santa Arianna until Aiden was killed in a car crash in 1949.

Arianna stayed in the home until her death in 1968, and she never remarried. Her children were given their inheritance, with the wish that the orchards be donated to the city.

In 1979, the city changed its name to Rancho Niguel. The Vineyard was eventually sold by the family, and the home was later sold in 1982 to the city.

Arianna and Aiden's three children have passed on, but she has four grandsons, two granddaughters, and eight great-grandkids remaining. The family sent a letter to the city pleading to have the home spared and saved. One of the great-grandkids just wrote a book about the whole story, and I can't wait to read it.

"I'm going to ask the Packard family to be a part of the celebration when we save this old gal." Roxy commented.

"I think that's a wonderful idea."

When we left the mansion, I dropped Roxy off at her place and headed home. I had about ten messages on my voicemail: Oliver and Martin, Jessica, Mrs. Green, Matt, Sara, Kiana, and even Sonya took time to call from her Mexican vacation.

Martin left a message saying, "Nikki, it's all over social media."

I took an ice pack from the freezer and put it on my cheek,

What a day!

Chapter 6

Maybe Margarita Ville

A week before the boardwalk opened, Chef Stark had a great idea: he thought we should rent out a space on the boardwalk to sell appetizers, desserts, and snacks. I thought he was a genius!

I had filled out the paperwork, put down the deposit and first month's rent on one of the snack stands, and we opened Kendle's Snack Shack the day of the boardwalk grand opening.

Sara had volunteered to take two shifts from her full-time hostess position at the restaurant to work on the boardwalk. I figured that it also didn't hurt that her boyfriend Jagger, was working at one of the lifeguards' stands. They would be able to see one another more often or have lunches together. Ah, young love!

Today, I was managing the snack stand. I put on a pair of white denim shorts and a light blue polo in the same color as our server's button-down shirts at Kendle's. I put my hair in a ponytail and off I went to open this late morning. Our hours here on the boardwalk were 11 am to 8 pm.

This morning, Sara and two of my younger cooks were on staff with me. Sara and I were at the register and the cooks, well, you know, were cooking in the back. We kept the snack menu simple,

Mini Sliders with cheese

Coconut shrimp on a stick with a choice of three dipping sauces

A four-cheese grill

Steak Street tacos with mango salsa

Chicken kabobs

Our sides -

French Fries, regular or truffle

Onion rings, beer battered

Fried mozzarella with a side of marinara

A garden salad with a choice of dressing

Popcorn butter or truffle butter

Chips and salsa

Our beverages were cool too we opted for

Aguas frescas- watermelon, lemonade, and coconut pineapple

Along with Coke, Sprite, Root beer, bottled water, and mineral water.

Our desserts were very summery-

Three flavors of gelato-

Spumoni

Pineapple

Vanilla coconut

We offered slices of cake and pies, too

Strawberry shortcake

Hummingbird cake

Chocolate cake

Pies-

Lemon meringue

Key lime

Berry

We all had a chance to test taste all of these items and boy, did the staff enjoy that day.

The afternoon was hot, already 85 degrees and still climbing.

Sara and I opened the registers and took the day's first customers.

Later on, Matt came by the stand, Sara already had a strawberry shortcake in a to-go box for him.

"Afternoon ladies." He was dressed in his work blues, his name Captain Stevens stitched on the right side of his shirt.

"On your way to the station," I asked him.

"I had a meeting with the city manager, Emma, so I'm on my way back to the station. I thought I'd stop by. Say hello!"

"And pick up a slice of your favorite cake." I smiled.

"You know me too well, Nikki." I handed him his box of cake, and he handed me a twenty, but I waved it away.

"It's on the house, a thank you for taking me out on the boat."

"Well, thank you. How about I put it in the tip jar?"

"We don't have a tip jar." I smiled.

Sara reached over and took the money. "I'll split it with the guys in the kitchen." Sara made change for the money and ran it back to the kitchen.

"Would you like anything to drink with that?" I asked Matt.

"No, I'm good, but thanks. How are you doing after the Stacie incident?"

"Not my greatest moment, but I just couldn't let her bully everyone."

"I saw the video that one of the protesters took. You have a good left hook there, Ms. Ali."

He joked, referring to the great retired boxer Leila Ali.

"Remind me not to get on your bad side again!"

Matt smiled, realizing he was on my naughty list once.

"So any news about what happened to Hawk McGuire?" He asked.

"I haven't heard anything since I had Roxy lawyer up, Paul has been tight-lipped about it, and Craig won't tell me anything either. All that we know is that he was stabbed with a wooden drumstick."

"Roxy is innocent, that I know for sure!" Matt replied.

After Matt left, the snack stand slowed down for the commute hour between 4:45 pm-5:30 pm, so I took this time to take a break.

"Sara, I'm taking a walk. I'll be back in fifteen minutes."

"Take your time, it's pretty slow, and I've got it covered."

I waved and then strolled out down the way on the boardwalk. I walked past it but then stopped at a cute little retail store called *Maybe Margarita Ville.* It was quaint, beach cottage-like, the walls were painted watercolor blue with white shiplap on the lower part of the walls, dark hardwood floors, and white shelving complemented the shop on the lake essence. The shop was filled with gifts, bath soaps, lotions, candles, sweatshirts, and t-shirts that read "Love the Lake" or "Life is better at the Lake."

Some really cute coasters caught my eye; they were made of sea glass in green, light blue, and pink. They reminded me of the necklace Paul gave me when we first began to date. He was in Santa Barbara surfing, and he found some sea glass in pink. He had it set in silver and added a small diamond to it, and put it on a silver chain. I remember how much controversy it caused at Matt's housewarming party last summer. I picked up four of the coasters in pink and decided to check out the bath salts.

"Those are from South Carolina, they are just magic." The gal at the cash register told me.

The salts had scents from lavender to coconut and vanilla almond, it was making me hungry. I picked one out and decided on the vanilla almond. I also picked out a white T-shirt with

"Life is Better on the Lake" in black writing with a blue lake on it and a dock, and an oar.

I took my merchandise to the register and placed them on the counter.

"You won't be disappointed with the salts."

"I can't wait to try them," I responded.

She placed everything in ocean-printed tissue paper and placed all of it in a coral-colored paper handle bag.

"Ok, that will be 65.95."

I handed her my credit card, she processed the charge, and then said

"Nikki Rodriguez, you're the lead singer for Little Black Dress, and don't you also own Kendle's?" She asked.

"Yes, I do." I smiled, a fan! Yay!

"I saw the video of your incident with that mean woman. What was her name?"

"Stacie!" I replied to her question.

"That was it, I only remember her because I've seen her before, she was having a discussion with that real estate mogul a few days before he died." The shop owner reminisced.

She had my full attention, so I asked her:

"What was going on?"

"Oh, that Stacie woman, she was talking to that guy, oh, what was his name?" She was trying to remember.

"You mean Hawk McGuire?" I clued her in!

"That's it, yes, that man, anyway, she was having a conversation with him and then she got really mad and she was yelling and waving her hands and then she walked off."

"What were they arguing about?" I was on the edge of my seat, foaming for more information.

"I'm not sure, but she did say a few times that *the council,* and then she kept saying that he *better keep his promise.* I'm not sure what it all means." She dismissed.

"Have you told the police?"

"No. I guess it just slipped my mind until right now. I didn't really think it was anything at the time just an argument in public."

"I can put you in touch with the two investigators on the case if you like?"

47

"I guess I should, but I don't have anyone to cover for me, I would have to close for a few hours."

"They can come to you, I can call them right now." I told her.

She looked hesitant but then changed her mind.

"I should, I mean, after all, now the guy is dead, ok, can you call them?"

"Sure."

I dialed Paul's number, and he picked up on the first ring

"Hi Nikki,"

"Paul, can you come to the boardwalk quickly? It has to do with the McGuire murder. The store is called Maybe Margarita Ville. The owner has some information for you."

"I'm on my way."

Chapter 7

Calling Lake Patrol

Craig and Paul arrived in ten minutes, they walked into the store dressed in khaki pants and black polo shirts with RNPD police logos on the front.

They had their holsters on and regulation Danner black lookout tactical boots.

Paul had his signature black Oakley shades on those beach green eyes of his.

"You have some information for us."

Paul asked, removing his shades.

"You guys are in your casual uniform, what's this?"I asked.

"We've been out with Lake patrol, we got a tip."

Craig filled me in right away.

Paul glared at Craig, most likely because he was giving out information to *me.*

"This is Lynn Houston, she has the information."

Craig took out his small notebook from his back pocket and took notes.

Lynn recounted her story just as she told me a few minutes before. Craig listened intently, Paul looked bothered at the first mention of Stacie's name.

I'm sure he was tired of her constant outbursts around Rancho Niguel.

When Lynn finished her story, Craig asked her a question.

"Ms. Houston, now you are sure this was Hawk McGuire she was talking to?"

"Oh yes, I'm positive, because I know him from his billboard that is in front of the Rancho Santa Arianna Mansion and Estate, it has his picture on it." I silently high-fived Lynn.

Yes! Now we had a witness to put Stacie in the suspect pool and remove the heat from Roxy.

Paul looked from me to Lynn and then asked her, "Ms. Rodriguez didn't in any way sway your story, did she? Did she pay you to say this?"

What! Is he crazy? What is he thinking that I set this up because it involved Stacie?

Lynn was confused; she gave Paul a strange look and then said, "Oh, no detective I recognized Nikki from the video that has that woman slapping her and it reminded me of the day I saw her having this tiff with Mr. McGuire."

Lynn said matter of fact, she thrust out her chest and nodded to Paul as if to say that's the truth.

Craig was surprised by Paul's question, he cut in with;

"Paul, Nikki wouldn't do that! Besides, we should look at the surveillance video on the boardwalk."

"Nikki, can I speak to you outside?" Paul asked me.

"Ok!" I passed by Craig, but he shrugged his shoulders and watched us exit the store. The sun was going down a bit and the sky turned dark orange.

When we were outside out of earshot from Craig and Lynn, he started with...

"You called me over here because it had to do with Stacie, didn't you?" Paul scolded me.

"I beg your pardon! I had some information about your case that's it, the fact that it has your precious Stacie is a coincidence."

What was wrong with Paul today? He seemed like a completely different person.

Hadn't we agreed to a truce last month or was it all just a lie? He continued with this accusatory behavior towards me.

"I think you want it to be Stacie, so you're searching for anyone who can say something against her.

You just want to hurt her and tear us apart!"

"What is your problem, Paul? This isn't like you! You said you and Stacie weren't seeing each other. What's really going on?" I asked him.

He glared at me and was going to say something else when I came back with "Paul, it's me, Nikki! Come on, this isn't us!" I touched his arm gently.

He blinked a few times as if he got something in his eyes, and then he looked away. He almost stumbled but corrected it right away. He turned to me now with warmth back in his cool green eyes.

"Nikki, what are we doing out here?" He asked me.

"Paul, are you ok?" I asked with so much curiosity.

He took a step back, rubbed his eyes, and then said.

"Nikki, I don't remember coming to the boardwalk or what happened this morning."

He looked around us, wondering why he was standing here with me. I called Craig out of the store immediately.

"Paul doesn't feel well, we need to get him to a doctor fast.

I briefly told him what happened. Paul looked back at me.

"Nikki, I'm so sorry, I just don't remember saying that to you." He held my hand when he apologized.

"You were like a different person from the moment you walked in and saw me." I added.

"I'll second that too. You've been weird all day, dude!" Craig told him.

"Let's go, Craig, I need to see my doctor."

Paul came back to his senses now.

"I'll call you later, Paul."

He waved to me with a smile, and I knew he was back to himself.

Chapter 8

Around The Bonfire

The next evening, Oliver had planned a big bonfire at the lake and said we needed to discuss the murder. I put on a pair of jeans and a white zip-down hoodie.

When I arrived the bonfire was already going, Mrs. Green stood with Martin and Oliver warming their hands. I set up my chair and joined them. Jessica and Roxy arrived followed by Tito and Daisy.

"Hey guys, good to see you all."

"I brought the stuff for s'mores." Daisy said, opening her bag of goodies.

We took out the sticks, placed marshmallows on them, and charred them away. After two very large s'mores filled with gooey roasted marshmallows and velvety-rich milk chocolate, I called this meeting to order.

"Ok, Nikki, tell us where we are with the recent clue on the case?" Martin asked.

I relayed what Lynn, the gift shop owner told us yesterday, and also how Paul wigged out and then didn't remember anything.

"It's Invasion of the Body Snatchers, isn't it?" Tito joked.

"Yeah, Stacie the body snatcher." Jessica replied, eating a gooey piece of marshmallow.

"Well, it does help my case, and you know what is weird, Paul had called me into the station again yesterday morning, telling me they had witnesses that saw me arguing with Hawk. I called Deidra, my lawyer, and she met me there. Paul *was* acting strangely.
He seemed different, more aggressive. Deidra told him he was on the border of harassing me. Me Roxy! Paul has never treated me like that!" Roxy said.

"Yesterday, you know I saw Paul in the lobby of Rancho General, he was leaving the hospital and he seemed fine, we spoke for just a few minutes and then he walked outside and I saw that Stacie picked him up in her new white BMW 7 series." Mrs. Green put in.

"He told me he was going to see his doctor." I said opening a bottle of water.

"You know something guys, I thought it was strange when Paul came into Starbucks for his usual hazelnut latte, but then he ordered something so different, he wanted an iced matcha tea with whipped cream!
He's never ordered anything like that, and he wanted a biscotti, he always goes for the brownies or the blueberry muffin, I thought it

was weird, but I just figured maybe he's on some new diet."
Jessica chimed in.

We all noticed that Paul was behaving very differently, but had no idea what was happening to him. Was he getting enough vitamins? Did he have a case of early-onset dementia?

Was he getting enough sleep? We had all asked these questions, and four of us had seen a different side of Paul. It was strange that we all had similar experiences on the same day.

"We need to get more clues! Martin, do we know anyone who works for that real estate company?" Roxy asked.

"I already thought of that, and no, we don't." Martin replied.

"Guys, let me ask Betty Jean, she's my general manager at Bella Rancho Realty, maybe she can give us some information."
I told everyone.

"I'm going to see her tomorrow night for our monthly card games, I can ask her."

Mrs. Green volunteered; she had become good friends with Betty Jean, along with Marge, and they had regular card game nights, sometimes bridge, poker, or even Texas hold 'em. I went to two card parties with these gals, and boy, are they fun.

"Ok, give me a call if you find out anything."

"Sure thing Nikki." Mrs. Green replied.

Oliver and Daisy brought up the incident of Stacie and me on social media, the video was made with the music in the background of "California Gurls" by Katy Perry. I was able to see it for myself, and it was crazy!

"Oh, man!" Tito shrieked when I hit Stacie.

Everyone was only watching our altercation, but I noticed something else. The assistant to Hawk! I had no idea what her name was; she left her seat the moment Stacie and I were escorted out of the building. From the video Daisy had, this angle was different from the other videos of our altercation.

When everyone went outside to watch us, the assistant and one of the council members, Rose Metcalf could be seen in the background shaking hands and passing an envelope between them. Hmm, what was in that envelope? Why were they so chummy with one another? Did I just witness a payoff?

Chapter 9

I'd Rather Be Surfing

The next day, I opened Kendle's Snack Shack with Sara and my two young cooks again. The sun was high today, 89 degrees, and the customers were coming in for the cool drinks.

The afternoon rush came between noon and 2 pm, we were slammed with kids, adults, and lots of teens.

Sara begged me for a tip jar, explaining that there was so much kindness in the hearts of our customers that we should just accept it.

"Really Sara, does this have anything to do with you saving for some wheels?"

Matt had told me that Sara's parents made her a deal, and she was required to come up with half of the down payment for her new car. They decided on a new red VW Jetta mid-level, and her share of the downpayment came to $3,500.00, plus the first six months of insurance payments. She had agreed, and she was $1000.00 short of her goal. She was hoping to get her car before going back to school, so she was motivated.

I had finally given in to her, she was so persuasive and nagging, she reminded me of myself.

"Nikki, I'm determined, I'm a hard worker, so I think it's acceptable to allow us to have the benefit of our wonderful customers' generosity."

"Sara, you are positively determined."

I cranked the music on our speakers, and Elvis was singing "Devil in Disguise"; it reminded me of one of those kids' cartoon movies (I think it's a Disney movie)with one of the characters, a little girl from Hawaii, and her pet, who was really an alien. After my thoughts ran from a Hawaiian Disney movie to Hawaiian dancing, it moved on to the trip to Hawaii that Paul and I were supposed to go on.

The tickets for the trip were for the end of June. I had given Paul that trip for Christmas, we were going to surf on some of the best beaches there. Then I thought, what happened to the tickets for the trip? I had prepaid for everything, it was a package deal I upgraded from Bon Voyage Travel Agency. I dialed the number of the travel agency.

"Hi, this is Nikki Rodriguez. I was hoping you could tell me if the tickets I purchased were ever used?"

"Hello, Ms. Rodriguez, let me look that up."

In a few minutes, and after some clicks on the computer keyboard, she came back with.

"It looks like the Hawaiian package was cashed in, we refunded the upgraded amount of money you added to the original raffle prize. It came to $8500.00, we gave back to Mr. Paul Anderson."

He took the money back! I felt like I was punched in the gut again.

"Thank you," I said.

I hung up the phone and thought for a moment. He didn't go on the trip, and he cashed it in. I wondered what he did with the money. It was bad for me to wonder; it was a gift, and whatever he did with the money wasn't any of my business. Although it was proper etiquette to return the gift or did it matter anymore? Nikki, you're so old-fashioned, I told myself.

My cell rang at that moment with the Kokomo song. I answered it without looking at the caller ID, big mistake!

"I just want you to know, this isn't over between us, Nikki!"

Before I had a chance to answer her, the line went dead!

I urgently walked outside of the snack shack and looked out into the crowd that was leisurely strolling the boardwalk. I looked from one end to the other, and then I saw her!

Stacie was standing a little past the store, *Maybe Margarita Ville.*

She gave me a long glare, her one eyebrow arched high, and then she smirked and mouthed the words "You're done!"

She walked away, putting on a pair of black Oakley shades similar to the ones Paul usually wore.

The breeze off the lake picked up, and now a chill ran down my back. Stacie was out for revenge. Right away, I dialed Paul's number!

"Hi Nikki, what's new?"

"Paul, I need to talk to you ASAP!"

He had been patrolling the lake today, he said they had a diver out under the area where Hawk was found.

They were searching for a missing brown leather messenger bag.

Some time later, Paul walked into Kendle's Snack Shack, his black Oakleys now on his head.

"Hi, Paul." Sara greeted him with a full smile.

"Sara, I didn't know you were working on the boardwalk."

"Yup, I'm helping out here and at the restaurant, but I get to see Jagger more here, and we get tips at this location."

She smiled with glee.

"I heard that you're in the market for some wheels."

"Yeah, I'm almost to my goal. Can I get you anything?"

"I'll take one of those coconut pineapple juices, and I need to speak with Nikki."

"Ok, one agua fresca coming up."

I heard Paul arrive, but I was on a call with Mrs. Green; she had some information for me. I told her I'd call her back and went around the counter.

"Hi,"

Sara gave Paul his drink. "That's $3.95 please."

Paul handed her a twenty-dollar bill. "Put the rest in your tip jar." He smiled.

"Thank you, Paul!" Sara replied.

Paul and I walked to the back, past the kitchen, and to a small office, no bigger than a small walk-in closet. We had one very small desk, a chair, a stool, and a laptop computer.

I closed the door, and he sat on the stool in front of my desk. I took a seat and began my story.

"I hate to bug you with this, but I got a very nasty call and semi-visit from Stacie."

"Oh no! What happened?" He asked, looking worried.

I told him word for word what she told me on the phone, and then when I went outside and saw her standing near *Maybe Margarita Ville,* the look she gave me, and what she said.

Paul took a big breath and exhaled. He was sick of Stacie's outbursts and all of the trouble she had been causing.

"Let me talk to her, I'll get her to leave you alone."

"Ok," Then I thought about what happened the other day and asked Paul about his health.

"Are you feeling better since the last time I saw you? You seem like your old self again."

" Yeah, I'm doing better, thanks."

"Are you any closer to finding the person who killed Hawk?"

"Like I said, we're out at the lake right now searching for clues."

"I might have one for you. Take a look at this."

I showed him the video of the fight between Stacie and me at the Rancho Santa Arianna Estate and had him focus on the background. "You see that!"

I pointed to the assistant shaking hands and giving an envelope to the council member Rose Metcalf.

"What do you make of it?" I asked him.

"I think if I were a betting man, I'd say it looks like a payout. I have to have proof, though. Let me do some checking into the council, and maybe I can find a connection."

"It would be nice not to have Roxy in your crosshairs."

"Nikki, I like Roxy, and believe me, I am doing everything I can to find the truth. My gut says Roxy didn't do it, but I follow the evidence, and the first thought when we found that drumstick under Hawk McGuire was that Roxy was the prime suspect. She is the one who led the protest against him, she had a public argument in front of many witnesses, she has written letters to him, not threatening but just very direct, and her opinion of him wasn't good. We follow the evidence, it's that simple! It's not personal!" He calmly stated.

"I know and I respect you for wanting the truth, but she's my best friend and I'm going to make sure she isn't blamed for something she didn't do."

"Nikki, you know me, I will never put someone away unless I have hard evidence that they committed the crime, an innocent person going away for a crime is the worst thing for a cop."

"Just find the one who is trying to set up Roxy and the one who is the real murderer."

"I will, you have my word."

Just then, his cell rang out.

"Craig, anything new?"

I could hear him on the line.

"Paul, you better get down here, we found the bag."

"I'm on my way."

"Maybe this will give you more answers!" I said, getting up from my desk chair.

Paul stood up to leave. "Nikki, trust me when I say I'm going to find the killer!"

He took a long drink of his agua fresca, enjoying the coconut pineapple flavor, and he said

"I'd rather be surfing right now."

He sighed, heading for the door with a dreamy look on his tanned face.

"Is that an invitation?"

"Yeah!" He smiled.

Chapter 10

Stacie's Place

I finally had a day off, I called Jessica and asked her if she wanted to do some sleuthing, but she said she was leaving for a three-day fitness conference in San Diego with her trainer/ new boyfriend. I had met him a few times, he seemed like a cool guy, Jessica said they had a lot in common, and if she was right, he would be the one! So next, I called Daisy and asked her if she was up to some clue chasing.

"Of course, Nikki, when and where?"

Daisy was more than willing to help, I picked her up from her and Tito's cottage by the restaurant.

Tito had gone fishing with some friends today, and Daisy was going to work a second shift at Kendle's, but I reprieved her of it and took a volunteer for the shift along with an extra two hours of double pay for that server.

"So where are we going, boss?" She asked.

"To Stacie's place!" We arrived at Stacie's apartment, she lived in the same complex as Paul, no big surprise, but this complex was huge, it may have been the largest complex in Ranch Niguel.

The apartments were Spanish style with red tiled roofs.

White stucco walls and rust color trim with lots of trees, beautiful fuchsia-colored Bougainvillea trees and bushes, and many plants in large waist-high colorful clay pots.

It resembled a hacienda hotel on the beaches of Mexico.

The property had four pools and four hot tubs, two clubhouses, five tennis courts, three gyms, and two basketball courts.

It was large and filled with lots of tenants, where no one really knew everyone.

It was perfect for my mission.

We parked in a visitors' spot and walked to Building T.

We were dressed in shorts and t-shirts with a beach bag over our shoulders, a pair of black sunglasses on, and plain white baseball caps. Blending in with no memorable description of two women walking around the complex.

We came to T101 Stacie's place, her door was hidden by a grouping of trees and a large flower pot in a corner, so we were hidden from any view.

"She's not here right?" Daisy asked me.

"I got it from Marge, you know her, she works in the mayor's office. Word is that Stacie is in a meeting as we speak with the Mayor, and then they both have a social lunch with the community business association, and guess what, Paul will be there too, so she is definitely busy for the next two hours or so."

I took out my lock picks and started to work the lock, and in two seconds, I was in. I know breaking and entering has become my specialty!

Daisy went in with me, and we decided to split up. I took the bedroom and she took the living room.

Stacy's place was cute, I'd give her that, the whole apartment was decorated in shabby chic furniture in colors of yellow, red, turquoise, and white.

I went into her room, she had a queen bed with a red floral duvet and matching pillows. In the corner, a small white desk sat.

I checked the three side drawers on the desk but only found blank paper, pens, a stapler, and some sunglasses.

I headed to the walk-in closet and looked around.

There were handbags a plenty, and a shoe collection I have to say I was a little envious of.

I looked in some of the shoe boxes but found nothing unusual there.

I returned to the bed and searched for a journal or anything she would put her most devious plans in. Nothing...

I went to the living room and asked Daisy

"Did you find anything?"

"No, it looks clean."

I looked around the room and then went to the bookcase. I found old high school yearbooks, paperback romance novels, art books, and a few picture frames. Some with her and Paul, ugg ...

I went into the kitchen with Daisy. "I can't believe there's nothing here."

"Let's check the cabinets and pantry." Daisy suggested.

We opened the kitchen drawers and opened cabinets, then I opened the door to the utility room off the kitchen.

Inside was a washer and dryer, the water heater, and shelving with fabric storage boxes in pale red.

Just when I was going to give up, I looked at the dryer, it looked off-kilter like it had been moved.

I took my phone and turned on the flashlight, and moved the dryer just a bit. Behind it, I found a file.

I picked it up and went to the kitchen counter with it. Daisy came up to me now and we went through it.

There were photos of Roxy and her apartment complex, a photo of me and Paul talking at the Harvest festival back in October, a photo of us at the Christmas party, and then photos of me at

Kendle's, photos of me singing, photos of Matt and me, it was getting scary how many photos of me she had.

We went through the file, there must have been about twenty pictures.

"She's obsessed with you, Nikki?" Daisy was scared now! The look on her face was filled with fear.

There was a photo of all of us at the lake, the most recent one, I assumed.

She circled me in red ink in the photo and wrote the words DIE! Daisy and I looked at one another. "I think you're right!" I told Daisy.

"Let's see if there is anything else behind the washer."

We went back to the utility room and moved the washer, and sure enough, there was another file.

It had all of the names of the city council, and there was an amount next to three of the four members with the word YES.

"Do you think these members have been bribed by Hawk? Did Stacie find out that Hawk had paid them all?

Is that why Lynn, the owner of the store *Maybe Margarita Ville* saw her arguing with Hawk?" I said out loud.

"That's what it looks like, maybe she has been investigating Hawk to protect the mayor." Daisy figured.

"I don't know, why would she develop a sudden conscience for doing the right thing?" I replied.

The next page had a diagram of the boardwalk, and an X on the spot where Hawk's body was found.

"She's investigating Hawk's murder, too! Maybe to impress Paul!" I said, taking out another piece of paper from the file.

"I bet she is, look at this, she put notes on the back of the page." Daisy pointed out

It read:

1. *blackmail*

2. *Roxy wrote damning letters to Hawk.*

3. *The council will vote for Hawk to purchase the property*

4. *Make a deal*

"It's hard to say what her intentions are here. Did she think she would confront Hawk and catch him in the act?" Daisy asked.

"Good question, maybe she thought if she had enough on Hawk, she could go to Paul, and then she would have broken a big case wide open. She would look like the hero."

I took out my phone and snapped some photos of all of the stuff she had in both files.

We put everything back in the files and put both of them back where we found them.

We went back to the living room and looked around.

"I guess that's all we're going to find."

I said disappointed. Just when we were going to call it quits and get ready to leave, there was a knock at the door.

Daisy and I froze!

The blinds had been drawn so no one could see us inside the apartment, but we stayed silent and still.

The person at the door knocked again. I went to the door peephole and saw Hawk's assistant Chelsey Hall. What was she doing here? She left after a few minutes, and I looked to see if the coast was clear.

Daisy and I decided to get the heck out of here!

Of course, I graciously tripped over a small side table, stumbling just a little, I gained my composure after a giggle or two, and moved on.

Definitely, a bruise will be there on my knee by morning!

"Are you all right?" Daisy asked, looking at my knee.

"Super!" I gave her the thumbs up with a stressed look on my face.

I opened the door, and Daisy stood as the lookout while I locked the door.

I noticed there was a note left for Stacie, Chelsey left it on the door knob. It was a yellow Post-it and it read:

"WE NEED TO TALK. CALL ME!"

I didn't touch the Post-it, just worked around it, and I relocked the door with my picks and put them in my beach bag.

Stacie was deep into something, and I was going to find out what it was!

Chapter 11

You're Engaged?

After I dropped Daisy off at her place, I called Martin and Oliver.

"Hi Oliver, are you guys busy?"

"Hey Nikki, I was going to call you, girl, we need to talk."

"I'll be right there."

I walked down to the mall, and in five minutes, I walked into Dunner Art Gallery.

"Hi, what's going on?"

"Why weren't you at the community business association luncheon?" Martin asked curiously.

"I had some other plans, why what happened?"

I now looked at both of them back and forth, waiting for what was coming next.

"Nikki, you missed it. Stacie introduced Paul as her fiancé!"

I was thrown!

What episode of the Twilight Zone did I just enter?

The room was spinning, and the words coming from Martin were slow and slurred.

"That cannot be true!" I yelled!

"Get her a chair, Martin, quick!"

Martin pulled a chair from behind the front counter and sat me down.

"Nikki, are you still with us?"

Oliver asked me, fanning me with a sheet of paper.

"I think she's coming around!" Martin stated.

Oliver went to get me a glass of water,

"Here, honey drink this."

I gulped down some water and came back to the conversation.

"I'm ok, I'm just surprised, I spoke with Paul a few days ago and he was nowhere near giving Stacie a proposal!"

"That's exactly what we thought, too!

Oh, believe me, everyone there was confused, there were a lot of whispers and finger-pointing."

"What did Paul say?" I asked.

"You know that's the funny thing, he looked right through me like I wasn't there, and his eyes were still and glassy, I got a weird feeling, Nikki." Martin said.

"Martin is right, I asked him away from Miss Psychopaths' ears, *Paul, what about Nikki?* Then he said *What about Nikki?* I told him *I thought you two were friends again,* and then he said *Stacie is the only woman for me.*" Oliver spat out, his eyebrow raised, and waved his hand to the side.

"Now, if that wasn't weird enough, CJ Groves acted like she worked for Stacie, it was strange, like she was under some sort of spell, her eyes were glassy too!" Martin said.

"Guys, there is something really weird going on!"

I told Martin and Oliver what Daisy and I found in the back of Stacie's washer and dryer, the many stocking photos, and I showed them the pictures I took of everything we found.

"Nikki, I sense another crazy here!" Oliver blurted out.

"You need to be careful, can you tell Craig? At this point, Paul is on another planet!"

Martin confirmed what we all thought.

"I'll talk to Craig when I get home." I said.

After leaving Dunner Art Gallery, Mrs. Green called me.

"Nikki, I have some news. Can you come to Bella Rancho Realty right now?"

"I'll be there in three minutes."

Here I go running again, what horrid news would await me now?

A few minutes later, I walked into the real estate office.

Betty Jean, Mrs. Green, and another woman sat at Betty Jean's desk.

"Hi, Ladies." I waved and pulled up a seat.

"Nikki, this is Lisa Carter, she worked at Hawks agency, and she has some information for you."

"Hi, Lisa."

I said, shaking hands with her.

"Nikki, it's nice to meet you, well, I wish it were under better circumstances."

"Yes, I agree."

"Lisa and I went to real estate courses together at the Rancho Niguel College, that's how we know each other."

Betty Jean told me. Lisa nodded,

"Betty Jean is a great agent, and I should have taken her up on her offer last year to work with her, but Hawk painted a fantasy of a picture, and I went to work for him. Boy, am I sorry I did?"

"What do you mean?" I asked her.

"It all started out okay, we had a great team, and I thought I was part of a fantastic work environment, but after three months, that all changed. Hawk became obsessed with the Rancho Santa Arianna property, he went right to the mayor and took a meeting about purchasing the old mansion.

He dined with the mayor and gave her some pretty lavish gifts, too." Lisa stated.

"That could be seen as a bribe, right?" I asked.

"Oh, I thought that at first too, but then he started getting anonymous letters, and then someone started calling him all of the time, and he would take the call in his office, and he would yell, the only thing I really heard was,

You can't do this to me?

Then, after about a month, he was fine.

The next thing we know, he's told all of us that when he acquires the property and builds the condo complex, we can purchase one for a discount.

I mean, the council hadn't even voted yet, and he had the contractor already paid to start demolition at the end of August. I saw the receipt!" Lisa said.

"Lisa, by any chance did you get a copy of it?" I asked her hoping.

"I did get a snapshot of it."

She pulled out her phone and showed me the invoice and the receipt that had PAID IN FULL printed on it with two signatures, the contractor's and Hawk McGuire's!

"Lisa, did you ever deal with this woman?"

I showed her a photo of Stacie.

"Yes, she came to the office a few times too, Stacie something."

Lisa couldn't remember her last name.

"Stacie McDaniels" I told her.

"Yes, that's it." Lisa replied.

"Why did she come by to speak with Hawk? Did he say why?"
I asked her.

"He just told us that Stacie was public relations for the mayor and that they were working together."

I relayed the fact that Stacie was seen arguing with Hawk, but Lisa said she never saw a disagreement between the two of them.

"Lisa, what do you know about Hawk's prior real estate acquisitions?" I asked her.

"Not much, but I can ask around for you, I still have lunch with some of the crew that works for the agency, they can't stand it too!"

She replied with a sour look on her face.

"Ok, thank you." I told her.

Lisa was a big help in narrowing down the fact that Stacie was up to her neck in having many meetings with Hawk.

I offered Lisa a position here at Bella Rancho Realty since she had left Hawk's agency.

She accepted and thanked me.

After Lisa left, I headed out, but not before I briefed Betty Jean and Mrs. Green about what Martin and Oliver told me minutes before I arrived here.

"Nikki, that can't be true. Paul would never ask her to marry him." Mrs. Green said.

"Of course not." Betty Jean replied.

They both said they would keep their ears open, and if anything came about, they would call.

I walked home. It had been a while since I had been to the gym, and my first thought was to go for a swim.

I needed to burn some energy. The pool at my complex had only two people: a teen girl and her mom, sitting on a lounge chair getting her tan on.

The teen was talking on the phone, just dipping her feet in the shallow end. Somewhere in the distance, the song.

"She's Not There" by The Zombies played.

I dropped my beach bag with my towel, my phone, and a bottle of water on a chair.

I dived into the deep end and swam a butterfly stroke.

While I was gliding through the aqua water, letting the cool rush over me, I thought of Paul.

I wasn't sure what was happening to him; one day he was normal, and the next day he was a different person.

Now, all of a sudden, he is engaged to Stacie?

My butterfly stroke turned into a lap swim, and I pushed hard, going back and forth, pushing the water aside, thrusting forward against the pressure.

My thoughts are going into oblivion at the idea of Paul taking vows with Stacie.

I swam as fast as I could, just like when I was back in college, soaring under the water, noises above me muted and almost non-existent.

I pushed on harder and faster, thrashing out like Jaws in the ocean, kicking and hitting the water with velocity. By the time I couldn't swim anymore, my muscles were hurting, and my chest felt heavy like a brick was lying on it, I came out of the deep end, water shooting out and droplets hitting the lawn furniture.

I climbed the ladder out of the pool.

My breathing was heavy and haggard, like I had swum against the largest wave in the ocean.

My one-piece black bathing suit clung to my body like a glove.

I leaned over, trying to catch my breath, with water dripping all around me, making a huge puddle.

"Taking out your frustrations?"

Paul stood in front of me.

I pulled my towel from my bag and wrapped it around me.

We were the only people here at the pool now, I sat down on one of

the lounge chairs, and with anger, I asked him.

"You're engaged?"

Chapter 12

Clear and Bright

Paul took a seat next to me, his eyes clear and bright.

"Nikki, I am here to ask you to stay away from me!"

The shocked expression on my face made him smirk.

"Are you punking me?" I asked.

"You know I'm spoken for, and although this is flattering, I'm in love with Stacie."

Now he was scaring me. What did he mean by he's *in love* with Stacie? Why did he look different? His expressions were cold, and his attitude was arrogant.

"Paul, last month you told me that the two of you were just friends. You said you were just trying to help her with her alcohol abuse, now all of a sudden you're ready to walk down the aisle with her!"

He stood up and walked around the patio table. I dried myself off and put on a black sheer wrap over my bathing suit.

"Nikki, I won't ask again!

Leave me and Stacie alone! If you see me around, just pretend you don't and walk on. We're getting married!

Why is that so hard for you to believe?"

He asked point-blank with a look of anger.

I took a step back, wondering who was inhabiting this man's body. He had never said these words to me with so much enjoyment in them.

I looked into his green eyes, clear and bright, and he was standing before me, but he wasn't there! Almost as if he was talking past me, it was strange, like he was in a trance.

He realized he came on strong and then softened a bit.

 "I'm trying to let you down easy, can you at least appreciate that?" He tried to tell me.

"Paul, I just don't understand. Last month, you were embarrassed by her behavior at Kendle's, and now she's the greatest person in the world! What's happened to you?"

I touched his shoulder, but then he walked away, leaving me crushed! Finally, I just said to him.

"Fine, goodbye!"

I took my bag and walked back to my place.

When I got home, I locked the door and went to take a shower...

The evening summer air was cool, I took a Modelo beer from the fridge, and sat on my patio sofa.

I put my feet up on the small coffee table and replayed the discussion at the pool with Paul in my head.

The large, bright moon shone gloriously above me, the midnight sky velvety and dark allowed the few stars I could see to gleam like small diamonds in a brooch.

Answers, I needed answers, why was Paul so darn weird, it's like he was possessed or he was being controlled somehow, maybe like hypnotized, almost like a zombie.

Then I thought about what Emma from the city substation told me, the mayor had behaved strangely, like a zombie, too.

What was Stacie up to?

After my lack of sleep the previous night, I called Roxy.

"Roxy, you won't believe what happened!"

I told her about my conversation with Paul, what he said, and his reaction to me.

"I don't believe it! What is going on with him? It's like Stacie is in his ear telling him what to say."

"That's exactly what I thought."

"Do you think she has any involvement with killing Hawk?"

"I don't know, but I think it's time to start looking at Stacie as suspect number 1 for everything. I *know* she was involved with the blast at Kendle's in February, and I know she had something to do with all of the incidents here in Rancho Niguel."

"What are you saying? Do you believe she was the one who let out the vampire information back in October or the one who leaked the heist from the Russian gun guys back in December?

What about the nail gun incident at the Community center? Plus, the acid on your car? Nikki, if what you are saying is true, that means that Stacie McDaniels has been the one sabotaging you since she arrived!"

"That's what I'm saying!" I told her.

"Then it's time to catch this woman before she gets away with it, and Paul."

Roxy and I decided to do some major sleuthing.

We agreed to meet up later tonight to follow Stacie and find some clues to her plan.

Roxy made some calls to our friends Oliver, Martin, Jessica, and Mrs. Green, and I went into Kendle's to speak with Tito and Daisy about what was going on since we didn't have time for a team meeting.

"Nikki, I think you and Roxy are on the right track here, but how are we going to find evidence that she killed Hawk or sabotaged you?" Tito asked.

"I know we can spy on her, maybe follow her."

Daisy chimed in.

"Yes, we need to see where she is going and what she is doing.

I called Marge, and she will give a heads-up when Stacie is headed out of work.

Tito, I need to borrow your truck for this. She doesn't know what you two drive, so I think it would be better than following her in my red Jeep."

"Absolutely boss!" Tito responded.

"I need you two to run things here at Kendle's tonight, Ken will take your morning shifts and manage.

I need you to tell anyone who asks for me that I'm in the upstairs office doing payroll and ordering our monthly inventory.

That usually keeps me in the office for at least four hours."

"Ok, we'll do Nikki," Daisy replied, saluting.

"Keep the lights on in my office, and if you can bring me a plate of food an hour after I arrive, that would be great.

I will make a few calls from my landline upstairs and then sneak out the back door from my office.

I'm going to leave my cell phone here on my desk, and Roxy and I will go old school and use walkie-talkies.

I also have two for you both, and we will be on Channel 3."

I handed off the two small radios to Tito and Daisy, and they slipped them into their apron pockets.

By 8 pm, it was dark, and our plan was in motion. Daisy had brought me a plate of food, which I gladly ate: beef Bolognese with penne pasta, and a side salad with a cold iced tea.

I changed my clothes from the sweet turquoise floral dress I had on to my black yoga pants, black tank top, and black windbreaker.

I slipped on my black Under Armor athletic shoes and a black baseball cap, my typical spy wear.

I picked up Roxy in Tito's black truck, and we waited for Stacie to get out of work. She walked out to her car with the mayor, and then she drove off.

I kept a safe distance so I wouldn't look like I was following her.

When we came close to the complex, I took a right turn and drove behind the complex and parked on the street.

Roxy and I moved quickly until we came to building T, and then we waited in the shadow of another corridor.

Through a small view between the trees, we saw Stacie turn the key and go inside her apartment. We crept next door to stand by. We saw her lights go on all over the apartment. Then we heard some footsteps and hid behind a large hedge.

Paul walked up to her front door and knocked.

Stacie opened the door with gusto and smiled like a small child with her favorite toy.

"Paul, come on in."

He walked in, and she shut the door. Roxy and I moved closer to the front window, still hiding but having a visual of the front room and the kitchen area.

Stacie and Paul kissed with a long, passionate kiss, then they sat on the sofa.

Ugg, I wanted to puke!!!

I pulled two stethoscopes from my backpack, and Roxy and I put them on. I got the idea last month when I was dating a doctor. Pretty cool huh!

It seemed logical, and this was our test of the product.

We placed the round flat part of the listening tool on the front window. With the earpieces in my ears now, I was able to hear their conversation, and this is what they said.

"Paul, I hope you had a chance to get Nikki away from you once and for all. She is the reason why we haven't been able to move forward." She said with a pout.

"Stacie, it was easier than I thought. She got mad, but she finally said goodbye to me for good. Now it's just you and me!"

Paul kissed Stacie with passion again! My stomach turned!

I had to endure this, and it was hard. Just when I couldn't take anymore, Paul pulled back and rubbed his head as if he had a migraine.

"What's wrong Paul? Are you having some pain?"

"I just need a minute."

Paul sat back on the sofa, his head fell back, and his eyes closed. In a few seconds, he opened his eyes and then said:

"Stacie, how did I get here?" He asked, confused.

He looked around, wondering why he was in Stacie's living room. He stood up right away.

"Stacie, I have to go back to work!"

The spell was broken! Stacie knew it, and now she was trying not to panic!

"Paul, could you just wait here for one minute? I'll be right back."

She got up from the sofa and walked to her bedroom.

Paul looked around, still wondering what had happened!

He pulled out his cell phone and dialed.

"Craig, I need you to do something for me. Can you come by the station in ten minutes? I need your help?"

He hung up and put his cell in his back pocket, he was walking toward the front door when Stacie reappeared. She held a glass of water and some pills.

"Paul, take these and you will be back to your old self in no time."

Paul took the pills from her and put them in his mouth.

"I have to go, it's about the case."

He turned to the door, and then Stacie pulled out an old timepiece on a chain.

She held it up in her hand and began to move it back and forth.

"Look at me, Paul, you are feeling relaxed and sleepy."

Paul looked at the timepiece, and now his body was relaxing, but then he shook it off and said:

"I have to go!"

He opened the door and slammed it behind him. Stacie began to yell.

"Paul, come back here!"

From our position, I had a clear view of Paul spitting out the pills in his mouth, he ran off to his car, now safely away from Stacie.

Roxy and I crouched down and removed our stethoscopes.

We put them in the backpack and decided to go.

"Let's hit it, I've seen enough!"

We got back in the truck, burned out, and headed back to Kendle's.

Chapter 13

A Case Of Hypnosis

Roxy and I reached the back lot of Kendle's, where I parked Tito's

black truck. We ran upstairs to my office. Roxy put our radios

away in my closet by the small spare room, and I called downstairs

to call Daisy and Tito upstairs.

"Boss, you guys made it back so soon, what happened?"

Tito asked anxiously.

"Stacie has been hypnotizing Paul, and giving him pills, we didn't

know what she gave him, but he spit them out when he left her

place, and then Roxy and I took off too!"

"No way, I didn't see that coming!" Daisy commented.

"We need to find out about Stacie's background, how does she

know how to hypnotize people. For all we know, she's been doing

this to the mayor, too!" I shot out.

"How are we going to find any information on her? Do you think

Craig will share?" Roxy asked.

"No, but I know who will, remember back in February when Paul's

friend at the FBI helped us with Freddie Santana's manager

stealing from him? Well, I am going to call the agent and see if he can give us some knowledge about Stacie Mc. Daniels..."

The next day, I was back at the boardwalk to open the stand with Sara and my two cooks. The sun was high in the sky today, and the lake was filled with boats and people having a grand time. I could hear the water skiers, inner tubers, and boats speeding around the lake. I went right to my small office and told Sara to call me if we got really busy.

"We'll do boss." She replied.

I dialed the number to Caleb Tores, the FBI agent friend of Paul's, who helped us out last February.

"Agent Tores, here."

"Hi, this is Nikki Rodriguez, I'm Paul's friend that you helped out with last February on the Freddie Santana case."

Oh, yeah, Nikki, the singer, how's it going?"

"Unfortunately, that's why I'm calling, I need a favor."

"Ok, shoot."

"I was hoping you could find some information about Stacie Mc. Daniels she has put Paul in danger, and I suspect she is responsible for a series of crimes in our town."

I gave Caleb the lowdown on some of the crimes we had suspected Stacie of and why it had escalated to full-blown murder.

"I'll do a thorough background check, investigate, and see if she is on any of our radars here. I'll get back to you by the end of the day, Nikki."

"Thank you, Caleb, again for all of your help."

"Thank you, the apprehension last February was gold to my office, I'll get right on this, Nikki."

"Thanks again." I hung up the phone and went back to work.

We were busy all day today with customers enjoying the sun, the lake, and the new boardwalk. I finally took a break and went to my tiny office. I went online on my AirBook and searched the term hypnosis. The definition I found was: *"a trancelike state that resembles sleep but is induced by a person whose suggestions are readily accepted by the subject.* The hypnotized individual appears to heed only the communications of the hypnotist and typically responds in an uncritical, automatic fashion while ignoring all aspects of the environment other than those pointed out by the hypnotist. In a hypnotic state, an individual tends to see, feel, smell, and otherwise perceive in accordance with the hypnotist's suggestions, even though these suggestions may be in apparent contradiction to the actual stimuli present in the environment. The effects of hypnosis are not limited to sensory change; even the subject's memory and awareness of self may be altered by suggestion, and the effects of the suggestions may be extended (post-hypnotically) into the subject's subsequent waking activity."

Courtesy of Encyclopedia Britannica online, thank you very much.

I realized that the state of Paul and Mayor CJ was that they had been put in a state of hypnosis. The next question was how did Stacie do this? And Why?

Chapter 14

"Cliff Side"

Today, being a Saturday, I called in some extra help, one more cook and another cashier to help Sara and me. Roxy showed up an hour later, and we all managed to handle the lunch rush with ease. By 3:30 pm, Jagger came by and picked up Sara for her lunch break. The two of them had their orders of sliders and fries, with two large Watermelon aguas fresca made to go.

"You guys going out to the lake to eat?" Roxy asked.

The background music of "Cruel Summer" by Bananarama is playing.

"Jagger has a spot ready by his lifeguard station, isn't he romantic?" Sara sang out.

Roxy and I smiled. "He sure is. Have a good lunch."

"And be good, kids."

We belted out and harmonized the words into a song!

Sara rolled her eyes.

"Oh my God, you two."

She chuckled and walked off with Jagger on her arm.

About ten minutes later, Matt came by, he was dressed in navy blue board shorts and a white t-shirt with the words VANS in green writing. Along with a pair of black and white checkered Vans, the "Spicolies," I call them, because they are the ones Sean Penn wore in the movie Fast Times at Ridgemont High.

"Hey, ladies, I have some news for you two about Hawk McGuire."

Roxy finished up with our customer and then joined Matt and me on a bar stool.

Our seating was basically null, with the exception of a small bar counter that faced the boardwalk. I sat down next to Matt to hear his spiel.

"I had breakfast with Tank and Brinks this morning, and we were catching up on everything going on around here.

They just returned from a big fishing trip in Mexico. Man, retirement has been nice for them. So, anyway, they hadn't heard what happened until they saw the viral video the other day with Nikki and Stacie in that catfight."

"Thanks for reminding me, Matt."

I said, not wanting to keep rehashing that day.

"Well, let me tell you what they said. Tank apparently had his mom in this swanky old folks home out in Pacific Palisades, and for some reason, he had to move her because they sold the place to a developer, and get this, do you know who that developer was?"

Roxy and I were fixated on Matt's next comment, but we were impatient, and I blurted out.

"Who?"

"Hawk McGuire!" Matt said, finishing his sentence.

"Tell me more Matt." I demanded, in a nice way.

"It gets better, doll. Tank also said that the patient coordinator and counselor was none other than Stacie Mc. Daniels."

"What! Oh my gosh, so there is a connection with Hawk, but more than we thought."

I said, holding fast to my seat.

"That's exactly what I thought." Matt replied.

"Is there anyone we can get in touch with?

Anyone who worked with her?" I asked.

"Yeah, can we talk to her co-workers or something?" Roxy asked.

"I'm glad you asked."

He smiled, showing his pearly whites.

"We have an appointment to speak with the facility's former director tomorrow at 10 a.m."

"How did you manage that? Wait, what do you mean we?"

I said, looking questionable.

"I'm going with you, I want in on the team. Martin told me about your mystery investigation group."

"My mystery investigation group?" I asked with sarcasm.

 Okay, I guess if Matt wanted in, I couldn't tell him no, after all, he got us our biggest break yet.

"Ok, team member tomorrow at 10 am." I agreed.

"I wish I could go, I have to work, but give me the details, ya'll, all right."

Roxy stated getting herself a Coke from the fountain machine, pouting her full red lips. Matt got up from his seat.

 "I have to go, but tomorrow at 9:15 am I'll pick you up at your place." Matt said as he headed out the door.

"Hey Matt." I called out. I smiled.

"Thanks."

"Anytime, darlin'!" He winked and walked out the door...

Later that day, Agent Caleb called to tell me that he was on a plane to Oklahoma to bust some criminals, but that he didn't forget about me; he said he would contact me in a few days.

The next day, I woke up bright and early with the songs from my surf rock station,

"Secret Agent Man" by Johnny Rivers played.

I danced my jerk while I got dressed.

Yes, I like to dance around in my underwear, who doesn't?

I put on my new emerald green and white tie waist bustier from White House Black Market.

It has removable spaghetti straps and can be worn strapless, but today was business attire, so I kept the straps on.

I paired it with white high-rise cutout hem bootcut crop jeans from the same store as my blouse and some beautiful emerald green Brooklyn studded flat sandals. Check them out.

I love this outfit, I added some gold hoop earrings and a gold bracelet to accent the green and white.

My favorite purchase so far. Matt arrived at 9:15 a.m. He was in a pair of khaki pants and a short-sleeved button-down camp shirt in ivory from Tommy Bahama.

"I love your shirt, it's a tropical Dodger theme, so cool, you look like you're ready to go on vacation to Key West."

"Thanks, you look fantastic!" Matt told me with a quick whistle "Come on, let's go."

He opened the passenger side door for me and helped me in.

These big trucks, Matt didn't do anything special to it; just factory set and already high off the ground enough, and he wasn't one for overdoing it. We took the 210 freeway and headed to Pasadena, the place we were going to was Casa Canyon, located in the Eaton

Canyon area of Pasadena and Altadena near the San Gabriel mountains. We pulled up to a large single-story building with a circular drive and an alcove or covered drive.

 The hacienda-style building had a large lawn that was green and healthy. Flowers grew in fancy flower borders along the building, daffodils in yellow, tulips in red, violet, and pretty green and white striped awnings on the many windows. It looked darling, like a nice vacation resort with mountains behind it.

We parked in the visitors' parking lot and headed to the front double doors.

Inside was just as swanky, the lobby was cool and filled with natural floral fragrance from the very large vase filled with colorful flowers on a large round table in the middle of the room.

The lobby desk resembled a hotel front desk. White Corian countertops with a freshly painted pale yellow back wall and a middle-aged woman in a tropical print dress in jewel tones greeted us with a large smile.

"Good morning, welcome to Casa Canyon, how may I help you today?"

"We have a 10 a.m. appointment with Ms. Carol Manning, my name is Matt Stevens, and this is Ms. Nikki Rodriguez."

With his charming disposition, Matt introduced us.

"Yes, I see that, right this way." The receptionist replied after seeing our names on her computer for our appointment.

She came around the desk and led us down a large hallway, the place really looked like a four-star hotel. We were led to a room with many windows, looking out to the pool area.

A medium-sized table sat in the room with a small stone fireplace and two wingback leather chairs in a light caramel color.

Another flower arrangement sat off to the right on a short hutch Style buffet in honey-colored wood. The room was calming and cozy.

"Ms. Manning, this is Mr. Stevens and Ms. Rodriguez, your 10 am appointment."

The receptionist said introducing us.

Ms. Manning was a tall glamorous gal in her late 60s, with fresh honey-colored blond hair in a shallow bun and warm brown eyes, dressed in a pretty tea-length summer dress in colors of orange, yellow, green, and red in a floral country print, a denim jean jacket with the sleeves rolled up complimented the look.

She held out her hand to greet us, with pretty delicate gold bangle bracelets on her left wrists, a simple solitaire round diamond wedding ring in gold, and some small gold hoops in her ears.

She looked like she was going to a nice summer swaray.

It seemed like everyone here paid great attention to their wardrobe.

I liked this place.

"It's nice to meet you both, please call me Carol."

"Thank you for having us today." I replied.

We sat down at the honey-colored table, getting comfortable.

"Would you like some coffee or water, or orange juice maybe?"

"Coffee would be nice, thank you." I replied.

Matt asked for a glass of OJ, then we began our discussion.

"Well, I know why you're here, Mr. Tank phoned me yesterday and filled me in on some of the details.

He mentioned that you wanted to know about my former co-worker Stacie McDaniels."

"Yes, we would like to know what her responsibilities were and if she had anything to do with what happened to the adult residence in Pacific Palisades."

"It's like I told Johnny, um, Mr. Tank, I had the unfortunate privilege of working with Ms. McDaniels for about two and a half years at Cliff Side Adult Residence in Pacific Palisades.

Oh, Cliffside was a beautiful place.

We had three hundred small studio apartments overlooking the ocean, with two dining facilities, a small golf course, tennis courts, two pools, shuffleboard, bocce ball, bicycles, and golf carts.

We had a long list of old Hollywood celebrities who had retired there. We had a wonderful support staff, kind and caring folks who loved their jobs, we were like a family. Then one day, Stacie arrived! She was hired as a patient coordinator and as a counselor. She had just graduated with a psychology degree and a one-year internship at the VA Mental Health Services in Los Angeles, her credentials were impressive."

Our beverages arrived, and Carol took a moment before the receptionist left the room to continue.

My coffee was delicious, wow, I needed the name of this stuff. Carol continued her story with Matt and me intently listening.

"At first, she was kind and a joy to be around; she was helpful and managed to lead a winning team in our annual tennis tournament. We all thought she would fit in fabulously.

Then, about a year after she was there, we had a visit from Hawk McGuire, the big real estate tycoon, and the Hawk went in to kill his prey, I like to say. Hawk came to our facility with one of our board members and charmed his way around to everyone.

He brought in an offer to purchase the property.

He said he intended not to change anything, only that he would own the property but that Cliff Side would remain Cliff Side."

She took a sip of her coffee and continued her story.

"A few weeks later, we received a letter from the board of trustees stating that the property was going to be sold to Hawk, who had plans for a teardown of the property for a new condo complex. The board said that the current residents had to find other places of residency; they gave us 30 days to be out."

"Wow, that's crazy."

I said as I was shocked!

"That's not the half of it. What happened next is where it all spiraled. The wealthiest residents became investors of this new condo complex, and all of a sudden, they were giving millions of dollars for a block of 2% of the complex to go to residency for low-income seniors, a 10% share from sales, and first in line for a condo of their own.

We all thought that was a generous act and I was almost fooled until I realized all of the donors were seeing Stacie for counseling, they would go to her office, and then for the rest of the day they were like functioning zombies, their eyes were clear and bright and I know this they were somewhere else! They weren't themselves. So I thought it was odd that the ten residents who donated their millions had one thing in common: they all had sessions with Stacie. Two of those residents went broke; they ended up staying with family until they passed on, and their families have lawsuits against Hawk and his company for damages.

As for the rest of them, they never had the chance to purchase those condos because Hawk sold them to the highest bidder first and then told these people that their money was simply a charitable donation, not an investment. He laughed at the 10% sales profit share that they claimed he promised.

The contracts that were signed by these residents, which promised these wonderful benefits suddenly didn't exist.

I had a chance to look at the receipt for the donations, and that's all the paperwork stated, *for donations only,* yet the residents had their signatures on them, but didn't remember signing these forms."

As we listened, my jaw continued to drop.

Hawk had swindled millions of dollars from unsuspecting wealthy seniors, and possibly with Stacie's help, forced them to sign away their money under hypnosis.

These two committed theft, fraud, elder abuse, and many more crimes here.

"How many of those residents were left broke?" Matt asked.

"Well, two of them for sure, six others had a family member or a lawyer stop them before they drained their funds.

The ones who had family paying their bills here removed their loved ones and found a new place for them.

Tank, his mother resides here, and I assured all of my residents no one like Stacie or Hawk will ever try this again as long as I live." She said sharply.

"I feel awful for the families that had to endure this.

Do you have any proof that Stacie did anything clinically to these patients of hers?" I asked Carol.

"I have five of them that will go before a jury and swear to the process that they do remember and testify that they had symptoms of hypnosis. I also have a renowned Psychiatrist who has been working with these former residents to remember everything that she did." I smiled. I knew we had Stacie now!

It was just a matter of time before we could connect her to Hawks' murder, and then Stacie McDaniels would pay for her crimes.

Chapter 15

In The Garden With Mrs. Tank

After we met with Carol, we visited Mrs. Tank, Johnny Tank's mom.

We walked with her out to the garden, she was more than glad to see Matt again.

"Oh, Matthew, it is wonderful to see you again, it has been six months, I believe."

Sharp as can be, she stated with certainty.

"Yes, ma'am, it was the birthday party for your grandson James. I remember you danced the twist with him on the dance floor. "

"I was always a good dancer."

She smiled.

" Now, who is this beautiful gal here?"

She asked, turning to me.

"This is my good friend Nikki Rodriguez."

We shook hands,

"It's nice to meet you, I had the privilege of singing for your son's retirement party back in October."

"Oh yes, I remember you, Poison Ivy. I arrived a little late, but I caught the act and the dedication to my Johnny from the Mayor."

She was remembering the retirement party where we all wore Halloween costumes for the celebration held at the Gothic Cafe and Inn last October.

"Yes, it was quite a party!"

I said, remembering the evening we had caught the Rancho Niguel vampire killer, aka Donna, my former manager at Kendle's.

"You caught that killer, I remember, my Johnny says you're a real Nancy Drew. Are you working on anything new?"

"As a matter of fact, Matt and I are here to ask about Stacie McDaniels."

I figured I might as well ask her since we were here.

We walked around the garden at the end of the property for more privacy.

She stopped and turned to us, "I can tell you this, I saw her having lunch with that detective boyfriend of hers when she worked at Cliff Side.

He was at the retirement party, he was Batman, they used to date, and I spoke to him a few times.

He's a very kind young man, always so helpful.

Anyway, they had lunch one afternoon, it was on one of the picnic benches overlooking the sea, and he was breaking it to her gently that they were better off going their separate ways, but before he could finish his sentence, she became upset.

She yelled obscenities and threw her lunch on the floor, and then she stood up and she slapped him!

When he tried to leave, she threw her cranberry juice at him.

Finally, she saw a few of her co-workers coming out of the dining room to see what the commotion was, and she calmed down.

I went back inside, and I saw the detective leave, and that was the last time I saw him until the retirement party."

"I am aware of her violent streak. What happened after that?" I asked.

"They sold the place and we had 30 days to move and I came here, I saw her at the retirement party, but I had a costume on so she didn't know who I was."

After our discussion, Matt and I played a round of miniature golf in the garden area of the facility with Tank's mom. She won twice, she was competitive, and she calculated our scores in her head, a sharp one she was.

It was lunchtime, and she and her group of friends were happy that today was Mexican buffet day.

"Thank you for coming to visit with me, Matthew."

She gave him a hug and a kiss on the cheek. She hugged me, too!

"It's nice to see you again, sweetie, you have the voice of an angel."

She said.

She went to Matt and whispered something in his ear. He smiled and said,

"Oh, don't worry, I will."

He told her.

She smiled and said, "Bye, you two."

She waved and then joined her friends in the dining hall.

She was definitely a sharp gal, Matt told me she walks two miles daily and enjoys swimming aerobics with her friends.

I had asked Matt why she didn't live with Tank and his family, and he said

"Tank has asked her many times to live with them, but she said she likes her independence and her friends. I think she has a few admirers here, and she loves being on her own."

"An independent woman, I like her."

We got back in the car, and Matt asked me if I was hungry.

"I'm starving, how about lunch?"

"Sounds good."

We stopped for Mexican food too, a favorite place of mine in downtown Pasadena called El Portal.

We feasted on chips and salsa first, and then I ordered my favorite Cochinita Pibil, a traditional Yucatec Mayan slow-roasted pork dish from the Yucatán Peninsula.

Matt went with the Carne Asada, good choice!

"Can you believe what we heard today about Stacie?"

Matt asked after taking a drink of his Modelo beer.

"Truthfully, it doesn't surprise me! I knew she was bad news the moment she arrived. I know this sounds crazy, Matt, but I know she is the one behind all of the sabotage on me.

Right down to the press being tipped off in October about Cat's killer, to the press getting the story about the Russian guy who killed his employees, and to the sabotage on the Community Center, the attack on me with the nail gun, my car being damaged and the blast at Kendle's, now she's killed and the hypnotizing wasn't the first time for her.

She's a career criminal."

I took a drink of my Modelo, now enjoying the refreshing cold taste of this beer.

"What does Paul think?

Is he convinced about Stacie being more trouble than he thinks?"

"Matt, he's a victim too!"

I told him about what Roxy and I witnessed while we spied on them at Stacie's house and the engagement, and Paul coming to see me to tell me to stay away from the happy couple.

He was really blown away by what I told him. He shook his head

"So what do we do next?" He asked.

"We need to find out how she killed Hawk and why?"

After lunch, Matt and I headed back to Rancho Niguel. We caught a bit of traffic, so we enjoyed some tunes.

A mix of summertime songs beginning with some Red Hot Chili Peppers "Californication"

"So are you guys singing at the Trout Festival this weekend?"

"Yes, we will be there. How about you?"

"The department will have a booth there, but other than that, I will be a spectator."

We reached my place, and one of my favorite songs was playing, so I lingered until it was over. "Amber" By 311

"I forgot how much you love this song girlie.

I thought you were just sticking around for me!"

He pretended to be sore about it.

"Oh, you know I secretly love you."

I flirted.

"For sure girlie."

He replied.

Then out of curiosity, I asked him.

"What was it that Tank's mom whispered to you?"

He chuckled and looked into my eyes.

"She said, Matthew, you should marry this girl."

Chapter 16

Trout Anyone

Saturday rolled around fast, and this morning I was up early to get ready. The Trout Fest was today, and the lake and the boardwalk would be extremely busy.

I had a quick breakfast of blueberry waffles and four slices of bacon. (Heck yeah, why not?) I finished the yummy Kona blend in my favorite mug and then headed out.

For the Trout Fest, we decided to go with cute cropped pants in white with aqua t-shirts, and white Keds.

We looked like we were ready for fishing in the Bahamas; all we needed were bucket hats.

We set up on the stage in the park facing the lake, right next to the Rancho Santa Arianna Mansion.

With the boardwalk and the blue lake in front of us, we began with the song "California Sun" by The Rivieras.

The park was filled with adults, kids, teens, and senior citizens, everyone was here.

The outdoor market had farm-style booths filled with goodies, fresh fruits, vegetables, organic honey, fresh bread booths, craft booths, handmade soap booths, booths for the Girl Scouts, the Boy Scouts, the PTA, the PD had a booth, and so did Rancho Niguel Fire and Rescue.

Plus, there were probably ten food trucks with many varieties of food and desserts.

I looked around the park, scanning for Paul or even for Stacie, but I had yet to see them.

I spotted Matt with his team of Fire and Rescue at their booth, he was shooting the breeze, drinking a Coke, and chatting it up with James and Anita, the EMTs, and my good friends.

The sun was high in the sky, shining down. A scorching 93 degrees, a slight wind blew by occasionally to cool us a bit, but other than that it was hot!

It was during our next song that I spotted her! On the last bar of "Club Tropicana" by Wham

I saw Stacie walking over to the city booth that stood next to the Fire and Rescue booth. Stacie then walked up to Matt and began a conversation.

Matt, ever so charming, was smiling and carrying on with Stacie, and if I didn't know better, it looked like she was flirting with him.

He flashed a look in my direction, one of his smiles that always said Darlin', I'm working this.

I knew he was a detective in disguise, trying to find something to give me on Stacie.

The passing audience clapped for us after our song, and then we began another cool tune.

"Let's Get Loud" by Jennifer Lopez, written by and recorded by Gloria Estefan.

Emily played a horn for the song, and Roxy played some bongos next to her drum set.

I danced with some salsa moves to the song, getting applause, and now the strolling people were stopped in front of us, clapping their hands, and some even dancing.

I saw the lake patrol boat pulling into a slip and docking. Paul and Craig disembarked and walked across the lawn towards the police booth. Paul looked at me and smiled, Craig waved, shaking his head with the beat of the music.

They strolled to the PD booth and began a conversation with their fellow officers there.

I danced and finished our song with glowing applause!

We left the stage for our break, taking long drinks from our water bottles, Hydro flasks in white with the words little black dress printed in black writing on them. Something Taylor purchased for us, she said, marketing is the cornerstone for our band.

The next band went up on stage and played "Summertime" by WAR.

I walked over to the Fire and Rescue booth. Stacie saw me coming and walked away from Matt, and rushed to Paul's side, wrapping her hands around his arm.

She gave a sly smile before turning her back and leading Paul to a food truck.

I asked Matt right away, "What did she tell you?"

"I congratulated her on her engagement, and she told me that Paul wants to get married right away, they are getting hitched next Saturday at sunset, and then going off to Hawaii."

"What?" I was shocked. Was Paul really going along with this nonsense? How could he?

Matt saw the look on my face. "Do you think she's lying?" He asked.

"I think she told you so that I would get upset and try to make a scene.

Come with me, I have a plan, just play along."

I winked at Matt.

Matt and I walked to Kendle's food truck, where Paul and Stacie picked up their plates of seared trout with pineapple salsa and cilantro rice.

"Paul, Stacie, I just wanted to congratulate the two of you." I sincerely told them.

"I heard you two are getting hitched next Saturday."

Paul looked down, not meeting my eyes. Stacie, on the other hand, had a satisfied look on her face; no doubt she had beaten me, and to her, it felt like a solid win.

"Uh... Thank you Nikki."

Paul replied.

"Paul, I just want you to be happy, and I hope that you have those five kids you always wanted. I know you two will start a family soon, it's all Paul ever talked about."

I addressed Stacie now! Paul had a strange look on his face. He then said, "That's really nice of you, Nikki! I'm glad you're such a good sport."

His green eyes were dull with enthusiasm.

Stacie's smile lessened, and she responded with,

"Well, we haven't decided on that yet, but we will have all the time in the world, as I become Mrs. Paul Anderson next week.

I'm sorry it's a small wedding, so you won't be there."

She smirked.

"That's okay, Matt and I will be out on the water enjoying the sun and having much-needed time to rekindle our relationship, we got back together again, so you don't have to worry, Paul I'm not going to interfere with your nuptials."

Matt pulled me close.

"I just want to thank you, Stacie, now that Nikki and I are back together, I couldn't be happier. Paul, I guess you and I won't have awkward episodes anymore, good luck dude."

Matt planted a kiss on me. The look on Stacy's face was complete satisfaction.

Paul looked like he had been punched, and I realized he wasn't under Stacie's spell any longer.

We then walked off together with Matt's arm around my waist.

Matt and I got back to the Fire and Rescue booth, we sat down on some chairs behind the tent, and Matt asked me what had just happened.

"I wanted to see if Paul was under her spell, and I can tell you he isn't anymore. I'm pretty sure he's on to her."

"Well, she did enjoy rubbing your nose in it!"

"I know." I smiled.

"Paul looked like I sucker punched him!"

Matt said with enjoyment.

"You did good, Matt. Now I know that Stacie thinks she won, she will feel confident, and we can catch her when she least expects it."

Chapter 17

Sitting On The Dock Of

The Lake

I went home at about 9 pm, after another group mixer with the mystery investigation group, as Matt put it. Mrs. Green, Marge, Betty Jean, and Lisa had a chance to share information from earlier today, and they came to our group with some new ideas.

"Well, here is what we think, Stacie is trying to get Mayor CJ to screw up big time."

"Yesterday, Ms. Mayor made a fool of herself in front of the Women's League For Change organization.

She told them she didn't support the new homeless shelter that St. Mark's was building. She nearly got booed off the stage at the Rancho Santa Arianna Mansion.

Stacie had to go up and calm everyone down and reassure them that the notes got mixed up and that the Mayor must have had an oversight."

Marge said, and then Lisa added what she thought.

"I spoke to a gal that still works at Hawks agency, and she told me she overheard Hawks assistant Chelsey on a phone call telling the person on the line that she wasn't going to pay a penny more."

We all looked around, wondering the same thing, but Martin said it out loud.

"Stacie is blackmailing her now!"

"Yup."

"Yeah, I second that!"

"Agree!" We all chimed in response to Martin's words.

"I'm going to call agent Caleb Tores back and tell him to look into Stacie's bank accounts and tell him what we all think about what Stacie is trying to pull here."

"Nikki, tell everyone what we found out today."

Matt included.

"What happened?"

Jessica asked.

"Yeah, you both disappeared for a while!"

Roxy said.

"Here's what happened."

After my story and some added references from Matt, everyone thought the same thing.

"Boss, I think now she'll let down her guard," Tito said, taking a bite of his shrimp taco.

"Stacie came into Starbucks yesterday and she bragged about going to get a diamond ring with Paul."

Jessica mentioned.

"I think she wants to make the Mayor look incompetent. Then she can slide right into the Mayor's position."

Daisy said.

"I agree, Daisy, she wants more power, and what better way than to be the head of the city."

I added.

"Nikki, don't forget about the Mayor's position with the council on destroying the Rancho Santa Arianna Mansion; she might side with them, she *is* the final vote."

Oliver added, reminding us that the payout from the destruction of the mansion was the reason for the blackmail and the death of Hawk.

"Has Craig said anything about what was in that messenger bag that they found?"

Martin asked.

"Craig hasn't said anything. If any of you can get him to talk, be my guest."

I said taking a sip of my beer.

"Not gonna happen."

Roxy replied.

After the meeting, we all went home. Matt dropped me off at my place.

"Thanks for the ride, and uh, about today, I just wanna say..."

"We were undercover, you don't need to explain, Nikki, I like this sleuthing, it's fun."

He smiled.

"Thanks again," I closed the truck door, and Matt waited until I was inside before he drove away.

I was exhausted, I took off my navy full zip hoodie and kicked off my Keds.

I took a bottle of water from the fridge and went outside, and sat on the back patio sofa. I put my feet up on the seagrass table, closed my eyes, and sighed.

"I thought you'd never get home."

My eyes shot open to the familiar voice of Paul! He walked out of the shadow of the patio, he was standing by the side fence.

"How did you get in here?"

I asked him getting up now.

"With my key. Remember, you gave it to me three weeks ago."

He said, dangling the gold key from his keychain.

"What do you want?"

"Are you and Matt back together?"

He asked with so much concern.

"No!"

I replied, shaking my head.

"Can we go somewhere to talk?"

He calmly asked me.

We drove down to the part of the lake away from the boardwalk and the boat launches. Paul drove to the south end parking lot, and we walked to a spot with a small wooden dock.

The moonlight was bright, a full golden moon shone over the small waves in the midnight color lake.

We sat down on the dock and put our feet into the water.

It was cool and refreshing on our toes.

"You gonna tell me what's going on now?"

I asked, turning to him.

He settled in and relaxed, putting his hands behind him, leaning back and supporting his weight on the dock.

126

Looking tired but alert, he began his story.

"I'm not engaged to Stacie, I'm not marrying her." He replied with a direct tone in his voice.

"I'm playing her game to find evidence against her."

He was serious with a slight content in his tone.

I knew this was hard for him to commit to trying to take Stacie down when he had given her so much support and help; his kindness for her bordered on sainthood.

He continued with his story.

"I found out that she has been drugging me and then hypnotizing me in her apartment.

For weeks, I couldn't figure out why I was having trouble remembering where I was or why I was getting the cold shoulder from everyone.

I went to see my doctor that day, Craig and I went to meet you at Maybe Margarita Ville.

My doctor took a blood test to find out what was going on, and a few days later, he called me to tell me he found that I had barbiturates in my system.

It was a light dose, but I had never taken them before.

It all made sense, the blackouts, the loss of memory, it all screamed hypnosis, and I know Stacie can do that; she has a master's degree in psychology with a certificate in hypnosis."

"I thought hypnosis didn't work to control you, I thought it was more like a guiding light to change or to better cope with something."

I asked him

"It is, you're right, but Stacie has learned to pair it with meds, and she found a way to work around that. I don't know how she does it, but she has."

"Are we talking like spells or black magic?"

"No." He chuckled.

"I think she found a way to manipulate the practice of hypnosis."

"So, tell me something, when you came to see me at the pool to tell me you were engaged, were you under hypnosis?"

"Yes, that day I came to the pool to talk to you, I had come from Stacie's place right before, and I think she put something in my root beer because I don't remember taking meds from her.

After I left your place, I went home and slept for six hours, and then I called Craig, and he told me Jessica told him I visited you and told you I was engaged and to stay away from us.

So Craig and I came up with a plan for me to pretend to be under her hypnosis and play her game to find clues.

Craig has me wired up, and he has been my backup until we have something solid."

"What about the pills she gave you? Did you find those?"

"I've searched her apartment and I've come up empty, the only thing I found was some evidence behind the washer and dryer," Paul said, looking like he missed something.

I knew what evidence he was talking about; it was the same stuff Daisy and I found there.

"Does she have another office or another house or apartment, maybe a cabin somewhere?"

"I've searched and there is nothing else in her name, no other properties, no postal boxes, nothing."

"Maybe it's not in her name?"

Paul looked at me, the wheels going in his head.

"We checked under her parents' names and her grandparents' names, and still nothing.

Wait a minute, what if it's a place in the mayor's name?"

He thought quickly and then placed a call on his cell.

"Craig, it's me. Can you check on places in Mayor CJ Grove's name?"

Craig called back in a few minutes.

"Paul, she has a cottage on North Persimmon Way, it's right off the east side of the lake."

He told him.

"Can we get a warrant tonight? Try Judge Rosas, he owes me a favor."

"Sure thing Paul."

"Thanks, Craig, text me the address, and I'll wait to hear from you."

He ended his call and turned to me, his silhouette a fine chiseled Greek statue in the moonlight.

"Nikki, I just want to apologize if I've been a complete jerk to you. It wasn't me, and I'm sorry if I made you feel bad.

I also want to apologize for the whole Stacie issue way back from when she arrived, I really was just trying to help her."

He was genuine and kind when he spoke, I knew he was truly sorry.

He rubbed my arm.

"Can you forgive me?"

"Of course."

We got up, shook off our wet feet, and put our shoes back on, then got into Paul's truck.

The radio went on, and the song "Sitting On The Dock Of The Bay" by Otis Redding played.

"I can drop you off at home, I know it's late, and you're probably tired."

"No, let's go find some evidence."

I winked,

He smiled brightly and hit the gas, and we drove to the cottage.

Chapter 18

Check It Out

We arrived at the cottage by the lake held in Mayor CJ's name, apparently, it was her grandfather's cabin that he used when he went fishing. After he died, he left his estate, including the fishing cabin to Mayor CJ.

Craig was on his way with the warrant, and some black and whites were en route as well.

The outside of the cottage resembled a small cozy shack with no more than two bedrooms with one bath.

It had a small porch with a set of white rocking chairs, the cottage was a light faded blue with white shutters, and a wide three-step staircase that led to a white farm-style door.

It was cute, the front window was large and we peered in to see a small sofa, a coffee table, and two chairs, behind it was a kitchen, in yellow. I think.

"It looks like it's been occupied; it's in good condition."

Paul said, moving to get a glimpse of the place.

I took a seat on one of the rocking chairs, I looked out to the lake, and I could make out the lights across it at the Rancho Santa Arianna mansion.

This side of the lake was much quieter and darker, but it seemed so peaceful too!

Paul went to look around the back and disappeared.

I saw lights in the distance, two police cars pulled up, and a white truck, a locksmith called *Rancho Locks*.

Paul came back around and met up with the uniforms, Officer Ryan, and Officer Yu, my old pals.

"Detective?"

They replied.

"We have to wait for Detective Zane, he has the warrant."

Paul said to the officers, the locksmith waited in his truck.

After about five minutes, Craig rolled up in a dark cruiser. He got out and told Paul, "We got it."

He handed the warrant to Paul.

The officers, and now the locksmith, went to the front door, the locksmith pulled his tools, and in thirty seconds the door was opened.

Paul taped the warrant to the front door, and they went in.

I waited outside on the rocking chair, I had no business there; I wasn't law enforcement.

Craig nodded to me, "Nikki."

"Craig." I said still sitting.

They went about searching the cottage, furniture was being moved, papers were rustling, and I heard a few doors open, cabinets, and a shower curtain.

Then one of the officers, Officer Yu, said;

"Detectives check it out."

Craig and Paul scurried across the room. I peeked from the front door and saw them go downstairs from the kitchen, which was most likely a basement.

I waited patiently, feeling left out, so I just paced the porch back and forth.

Paul came back up and called me.

"Nikki, I need you to go! Take my truck and I'll come by later to get it."

"Ok, what's going on?"

"I need you to go, trust me."

He said, looking deep into my eyes, so serious and trustworthy.

"Ok," I took his keys and turned and ran to his truck. I started it up and headed home. I parked in a visitor's stall and went inside.

What could possibly be so bad that Paul had me leave?

Did he find another wall with photos of all of us? Were there red circles around the faces?

Did they find a journal?

A manifesto for her evil plot?

What could have been so bad that Paul made me leave?

Two hours later, it was about 3 am, and Paul called me.

"Nikki, we found a body!"

"Who is it?"

"Hawks assistant Chelsey Hall."

I nearly dropped the phone; that's why he had me leave, they found a body! Crime scene, yikes again!

The woman that Lisa said was arguing with Stacie, the one who said she wasn't going to pay a penny more!

Chelsey Hall, Hawks assistant! Now she was dead too!

"Paul, I need to tell you something!"

Craig dropped off Paul at my place ten minutes later. He came in and looked so tired.

I offered him something to drink, and he asked for a beer.

He took a long drink and finally came up for air.

"Ok, Rodriguez, spill it!"

I told Paul what Lisa had said earlier this evening about what her friend had overheard with Chelsey Hall. I didn't tell him we all gathered around the bonfire and exchanged ideas and plans, just that Lisa had given me this information.

He seemed okay about it. He finished his beer and then said:

"She was stabbed too, with a knife from the kitchen."

He said, looking forlorn.

"She set the mayor up!"

I replied.

Chapter 19

I Thought He Was Breaking In...

Here we go again...

Mayor CJ was the prime suspect in the murder of Chelsey Hall!

The cops found Chelsey's car parked down the road from the

cottage, her navy blue BMW with the license plate that read

#1RLTR (number 1 realtor).

Her cell phone was missing, so that was another tip that the killer

had taken to be disposed of.

I called Roxy immediately, and even though it was a little after 3

am, she picked up right away.

"Hey, you're not going to believe this? Paul and Craig found a

body in Mayor CJ's fishing cottage."

"What? How?"

 She yelled so loudly that I had to pull the phone away from my

ear. Paul raised his eyebrows in surprise.

"Just curious, are you missing any knives in your place?"

"Hold up, I'll check."

After a few minutes and some sounds of Roxy opening drawers

and some clamoring, she came back on the line.

"Nikki, all of my knives are here; I don't have any missing."

She said with confidence!

"She doesn't have any missing Paul."

Paul dialed a number on his cell.

"This is Detective Anderson. Did we get any prints on the knife yet?" I walked to the hallway to talk to Roxy.

"Wait, is Paul there with you? I thought he was under Stacie's spell. What gives?"

I gave her the Cliff's notes version of what Paul told me at the lake, and then let her know that he is aware of what Stacie is up to.

"Roxy, Stacie set up the mayor. I think I know what's going on, it's about making the mayor look really bad. She is setting up the mayor to make it look like Mayor CJ was trying to frame you to go down for her crimes ."

"Do you think Stacie is doing this to get the Mayor out of the way, just like what we talked about this evening?"

"Yes, I do!"

Paul put his phone back in his pocket and walked to the hallway.

"Hold on." I told her

"Nikki, there are no prints on the knife, but there was a note in the victim's shoe, and get this, it's a letter from Hawk saying that if he ends up dead, tell everyone that Stacie was blackmailing him!"

I relayed it to Roxy,

"Girl, this is getting worse by the minute. What are we going to do?"

"We'll think of something, keep Dedra's number close by just in case Paul needs to officially speak with you again."

"Ok, see ya!"

I hung up and sat back on the couch.

"When we searched Chelsey's apartment, we didn't find anything. I'll have to go to her office in the morning."

"Why would the knife not have any prints?

I mean, it looks like Mayor CJ killed this woman and didn't have time to get rid of the body, so she just left her in the basement? That doesn't make sense!"

"The coroner puts the time of death around 8:45 pm, and I dropped off Stacie at her place around 7:45 pm. That's plenty of time to kill her. "

"Why leave the body in the basement? No one would find it, unless she had another part of the plan, and she had no clue the police would be here this evening."

It still didn't make any sense to me!

He yawned and then rubbed his eyes and pinched the bridge of his nose. I knew he was tired!

"Now, no arguments, you are not driving home, you need to hit the hay and get some sleep."

He didn't object and took my advice.

Paul was used to working very odd hours and therefore kept a duffel bag in his truck with clean clothes, toiletries, and shoes. He went to the truck to get it, then brushed his teeth, and crashed on the couch in his boxers.

My air conditioner was set to 67, so I covered him with a cotton sheet and a thin coverlet. He looked so tired, he slept flat on his back, his muscled chest lightly rising up and down, and his arms to his sides.

I said goodnight and I went back to my room, to go to bed myself and turn off the day's events, peace and quiet at least for a few hours.

The next morning, I woke up around 10 am, I went in for a shower, and just as I was getting out and putting on my robe, I heard some shouting.

I ran into the living room, and Matt and Paul had angry looks and glares on their faces; they both had swollen cheeks, too!

Oh boy, what kind of chicken fight happened now?

"What is going on?" I asked. Paul was still only dressed in his boxers.

"I thought someone was trying to break in."

"I thought someone broke in." They both said this at the same time

"What are you doing here Matt?" I asked.

"I came by to bring you some breakfast and to talk to you about Roxy and her case. What's he doing here?"

Matt asked, looking over at Paul with the stink eye.

"She doesn't have to answer that!" Paul spat out at him.

"Well, for one thing, it's none of your business; this is my place."

I told Matt with my hands on my hips, in my short cotton aqua floral robe, with my dark wet hair dripping on my wood floors.

"I was asleep when I heard the lock turn, and then I went into cop mode."

Paul said, explaining his side of the scenario!

"I opened the door with a key,"

Matt replied sarcastically.

"You could have opened the door with lock picks for all I knew, I was half asleep, man!"

Paul shot back!

"So the two of you jumped each other."

I smiled and then giggled.

They both said nothing, just shook their heads.

I went to the icebox, removed some cold packs, and handed each one a cold compress for their bruised egos, I mean, bruised cheeks.

"Ok, I'm going to finish getting ready, you two work it out!"

I said, keeping a smile from my face.

"I'm outta here,"

Matt said, placing the cold pack on the breakfast bar.

"That's a good idea,"

Paul remarked, making his way to the kitchen sink.

I went back to my room to change and dry my hair.

It's a good thing I'm single!

Chapter 20

News From Agent Tores

After I got dressed, Paul went in for a shower, and I tore into the pastries that Matt brought.

I made some French press coffee and poured a cup, then I went outside to the patio sofa. I indulged in one chocolate doughnut and one cheese Danish.

I got a call from Roxy, so I answered it right away.

"Hey girl, what happened over there at your place? Matt called me and told me Paul spent the night there and they punched each other."

"It was a misunderstanding, they both thought the other was a break-in in so they just about beat each other.

If you ask me, I think they both made that excuse to hit one another." I told Roxy.

"Wow! I thought the catfight between you and Stacie was bad, but man, I wish I could have seen that!

It almost made me forget about the murders."

Roxy chuckled,

"Nothing happened. Paul was really tired last night, so I made him sleep on the sofa.

Then Matt barged in this morning, and I'm sure got the wrong idea.

All that it means is that I need to make it clear that I'm single right now and nothing romantic has been going on!"

I heard Paul going into the kitchen, "Roxy, let me call you back."

"Ok!" She then hung up.

Paul came out with his cup of coffee and a glazed doughnut, and he sat down beside me.

His fresh, clean aftershave in the air made it hard to resist wanting to kiss him. Oh man, why did I have the Paul bug again?

No romance, Nikki. Remember back in February when you were dumped by him?

My inner voice said.

"Thank you for letting me crash here. I'm sorry about this morning."

He said, then took a sip of coffee.

"It's no biggy."

I waved my hand dismissing it.

"How is this whole thing going to end?" I asked him.

Just then, my cell rang. It was Agent Tores with the FBI.

"Hello."

"Nikki, I would have called sooner, but my team was away from the local office."

"No problem, so is there anything new?"

"I did run a search in our database for Stacie McDaniels, and I got a hit."

"Paul is here with me, can I put you on speakerphone?"

"Sure."

"Ok, go ahead," I told him.

"Hey, Paul."

"Caleb, good to hear from you."

"I got some intel on Stacie, our office has been investigating her involvement in the affairs from a 65+ senior home out in Pacific Palisades called Cliff Side.

It appears that multiple former residents there had been scammed out of their retirement savings or their family money."

I already had this intel thanks to Matt and our meeting with Carol, the former residence manager and now head of the new residence in Pasadena, where Tank's mom was living.

However, I listened in with great enthusiasm.

"We have witnesses that say Stacie used hypnosis to manipulate their understanding of investing money in a developer that tore the place down and built some ritzy condos there.

To their surprise, it wasn't an investment but rather a charity donation, they were out a lot of money.

The families are in lawsuits with the former Hawk McGuire and holdings, as far as Stacie, some witnesses will testify, but we don't have her on any of the other crimes that Hawk committed.

We had a Swiss account that turned up in Stacie's name, but it was recently closed, and we haven't found any other bank accounts here or offshore in her name.

So, other than that, there's no smoking gun on her. What we need is a paper trail for her crimes, maybe contracts between Hawk and her, payment receipts, or a confession from her.

At this time, we don't have anything else."

"Caleb, I think she has a place where she's stashing everything. We also have two dead bodies that are possibly connected to her. We just found a letter allegedly written by Hawk McGuire, and he implicates Stacie as a blackmailer."

"Have you tested it yet, prints and handwriting?" Caleb asked.

"In the process, as we speak, I can give you a call as soon as we know."

"Ok, Paul, I'll be waiting for your call."

"Sounds like a plan."

I hung up my phone, and Paul stood up and finished the last of his coffee. We went back inside and put the dishes in the sink.

"Are you going to have Stacie brought in for questioning today?"

"We decided not to let her know that she is a suspect, to keep her feeling secure, and this way she won't bolt.

We can gather more evidence that way.

It's good what you did yesterday, making her believe that you and Matt were back together. She was really in a good mood, so if you see me around her today or tomorrow, don't take anything I say as the truth. I'm undercover, ok!"

"Ok, I understand. A covert operation here." I said being a little silly. He took his tote bag and headed for the front door.

He seemed quiet and a little distant right now.

"Paul, are you ok?"

I asked him with concern. He put down his bag and turned to me, "It was a hard pill to swallow. I was at her place, and she went out for a few minutes to get a few things from the store across the street. I had told her I had a hard day and I needed a nap.

After she left, I started looking around, searching for something, anything that would give me some answers!

147

Then I saw what she had behind the dryer.

The photos I found were disturbing, and I realized she has been ill for a while now, and it wasn't just the alcohol; it was much more. Now I need to make sure I protect everyone from her, I know she was most likely responsible for everything right when she arrived, the vampire theory leak, the tip-off to the press about the gun shop, the sabotage at the community center, the nail gun incident, your car, and the one that gets me the explosion at Kendle's.

She's not the person I once knew."

He was disappointed in himself for not seeing this before or for believing me.

"I'm sorry, Nikki, I should have listened to you early on, I guess I just didn't want to believe it."

"I know, it's difficult to know that someone you trusted has been up to so much crime. Sometimes we don't want to believe that someone we once loved can be so damaging." He accepted what I said and agreed with me.

"Again, for what it's worth, I'm sorry, but you have my word I'm going to stop her."

"I know."

He smiled sweetly, and he left.

Chapter 21

Say It Again Jagger

News of Chelsey Hall being found murdered in the Mayor's lakeside cabin filled the community today.

The local news had a story on it as well as the paper, the bloggers, the local podcasters, and the patrons of the crowded coffee houses.

Gossip and theories were heard all over town, and everyone was now shining the spotlight on Mayor CJ Groves.

I caught a snippet of the local news on TV and saw her being ushered into the police department, with a few bodyguards and reporters gushing all around her.

I didn't have time to talk to Jessica, I picked up my mobile order, and I told her I would call her later.

I arrived at the boardwalk early to get into Kendle's Snack Shack to go over some paperwork.

Sara and my two cooks would be here in an hour, so I had some time for investigating too!

I pulled out my notebook and added some clues,

Chelsey Hall- found in the basement of the Mayor's fishing cottage

Time of death - approximately 8:45 pm

The body was found at 10 pm

A note was found implicating Stacie of blackmail

Swiss account in Stacie's name closed!

Money?

Where is the money?

I was thinking about these clues. What was Stacie's motive?

I wrote down in my notebook

Motives

She needs power

She wants the mayor's position

She wants Paul

She wants money

These motives seemed great, but which one? Maybe all of the above? Today's lunch rush on the boardwalk was busier than usual. Sara and I hustled all day, and by the time we closed, we were exhausted.

Plus, her tip jar grew to the size of a gallon jug, and it was filled to the brim with green.

Sara was getting a ride with Jagger, who was waiting outside for her, wearing his red lifeguard regulation shorts and his white t-shirt with the words LIFEGUARD OF RANCHO NIGUEL, with the Rancho Niguel crest on the front pocket.

I put my bag over my shoulder and we made our way to the end of the boardwalk while discussing the case.

"I still can't believe they found a body at the Mayor's cottage. You don't think she actually killed this woman, do you, Nikki?"

"No, Sara, I don't think the mayor did it."

"She doesn't seem like a killer! I'll tell you who I don't like is that assistant of hers that's always bugging Paul and being gritty with you." Sara responded.

I didn't want to tell her everything I knew because I was hoping to keep her safe; the less she knew, the better.

Sara was the type who would go sleuthing and drag poor Jagger with her.

She was a very concerned type who had a knack for finding the truth.

"That lady who hangs with the mayor."

Jagger commented as he tried to remember something; he was thinking and turning the ideas in his head.

"Now I know where I saw her, she was hanging around the mansion.

When my shift ended and us guys were all headed back to our cars, we were messing around with my bro's skateboard and we were recording him riding it around the parking lot doing tricks. Anyway, I remember thinking that it was weird that she was alone, walking to the side of the mansion when it was dark. Is there another entrance on the side of the house?"

Jagger asked

"I don't know, but that's a very interesting observation, Jagger. What happened next?"

"Oh yeah, well, some lady called out her name and she walked back to the front of the mansion and they both met up at the fountain in front of the house and then I headed off, that's all I saw."

"What day was this?" Sara asked him.

I was thinking the same thing, but Sara beat me to the question.

"Yesterday," Jagger responded.

"Who was the other lady?" I asked.

Sara and I were now excited for answers from Jagger.

"She was um, oh man!"

He ran his hand through his short hair.

"It was that lady who was just killed, Chelsey something."

He trailed off, "Chelsey Hall?"

"Yeah, yeah, that lady. Crazy huh?"

He remarked, astonished by his realization.

"Around what time?" I asked.

"Maybe like 8 o'clock."

"Jagger, I need you to go to the police department and tell Paul and Craig what you just told me.

Jagger, you said you had a video of your friend doing tricks. Can I see that footage?"

Jagger handed me his iPhone and played the video of his friend doing tricks on his skateboard, and behind them was the mansion and a visual of Stacie and Chelsey Hall having a discussion right in front of the mermaid water fountain.

The time stamp of the video read the night Chelsey died, and the time stated it was 8:03 pm.

"We are going to need this, Jagger."

"Sure. Is it important?"

"Yes, Jagger, you need to get this video and your statement down so it's official; you might have just saved the mayor from being accused of murder."

"Far out!" Jagger remarked, looking like a kid who just saved a cat from a tall tree.

"I'll go with you, come on, Jagger. Wait, what about you, Nikki, are you coming with us?" Sara asked me.

"I'm right behind you."

Chapter 22

Help Me Nikki!

Sara, Jagger, and I arrived at the station quickly, where we were practically running into the lobby.

"I need to speak with Detective Anderson or Detective Craig Zane immediately."

I blurted out to the officer behind the lobby front desk of the police department, I think his name was Officer Todd. One of those names where he had two first names, I read his nameplate H. Todd. That's right, his first name is Henry.

"Whoa, slow down, Nikki, they are interviewing the Mayor right now, and I'm not going to disturb them." The officer replied.

"This has to do with the Mayor, it may clear her, but we must speak to them, please." The officer nodded yes, "Ok, I'll be right back."

He went to the back offices to relay my message to Craig and Paul.

"Ok, guys, it looks like we will be speaking to Paul soon."

I assured Jagger and Sara.

"Wow, Ms. Nikki, all of the officers know you."

Jagger smiled with enthusiasm.

"That's how it is when you've dated a detective." I chuckled.

Just then, the officer came back with Paul.

"Nikki, Officer Todd gave me the message. What's going on?"

Paul looked so handsome in his dark jeans and white button-down shirt. His blue-ish green tie gave a cool summer essence to his ensemble.

"Paul, Jagger has some eyewitness accounts of Stacie and Chelsey meeting just an hour before her murder."

I told him while bringing Jagger forward by the shoulders.

"Is this true Jagger?" Paul asked him.

"Yes, sir, I witnessed Stacie and Chelsey meeting at the mansion at around 8 pm the night she died, sir. I also have a video of their meeting." Jagger was forthcoming and very honest with his reply.

"Come on back, I need to take your statement, and I'll take a look at that footage. Nikki, if you and Sara can wait here, I need to interview Jagger; just give us fifteen minutes."

Paul asked while ushering Jagger to the door.

"I'll be right here, Jagger." Sara responded

"Thanks, Paul." I replied with a smile of gratitude.

He smiled back with those gorgeous green eyes, and of course, I became glassy-eyed and just smiled.

Silently I smacked my ass! Oh, no, bad Nikki was back! No more romance! Aye Yai Yai, girl, what is wrong with you?

Last week, it was Matt you were drooling over.

Stop making it difficult, you can't, and I mean you can't be head over heels with two hotties.

It's not allowed. Well, for one thing, I'm not dating.

There is nothing wrong with flirting, I'm not married, and I'm not even in a relationship with either one.

What's wrong with innocent flirting and long smiles of pure romantic bliss? After my inner argument with myself, Sara and I took a seat in the lobby.

"Nikki, do you think Jagger could give the Mayor an alibi or maybe even keep her from being the suspect and put Stacie as the one who did this horrific crime and all of the stuff that happened to you, too?"

"I hope this can do that. Stacie needs to go down; she has committed too many crimes, and yes, you're right, she is responsible for all of the chaos and sabotage on me."

"Even the blast at Kendle's?"

Sara's eyes were wide with amazement.

"Yes, Sara, even that one she's responsible for."

Sara put her hand to her mouth in shock.

"Nikki, you were almost killed that day."

"I know." I nodded.

"This Stacie, is she going to come after you again Nikki or what about Paul? Is he safe?"

She asked, genuinely worried for us.

"Well, if we can get all of the evidence in line and find the smoking gun, she's going away for a long, long time."

"So are you and Paul good, I mean, is he still loyal to her or what?" I didn't want to blow Paul's cover, but I needed to reassure Sara that Paul was fine.

She liked Paul and thought he was a fantastic guy. She confided this to me a few weeks ago, along with telling me she would love nothing more than if we became family, a real sister-in-law.

I had told her to put on the brakes, and that I wasn't anywhere near that. She did tell me, "Nikki, no matter which guy you pick, promise me we will always be sisters."

I told her, of course, Sara, sisters for life.

"Paul can take care of himself, he's a good guy and a good cop, don't underestimate him."

I smiled to keep it cool.

"I agree, you're right, Nikki." She relaxed.

When Jagger reappeared, she ran to him and gave him a big hug.

"So is everything cool?"

She asked Jagger, but directed it more to Paul.

"Don't worry Sara, Jagger gave us a direct timeline, and with the video, it clears the Mayor. She was home during that time; she was on a landline speaking with the Mayor of Westwood, and that has been confirmed.

Also, there's the fact that where the mayor's mansion is, it would have been difficult to get to the lake house by the time Chelsey was killed.

The evidence has moved away from the Mayor, so it looks like we are on to another suspect.

Mayor CJ will be out in a few minutes with her lawyer. She wants to thank Jagger, and she wants to speak with you, Nikki."

"Sure."

Sara and Jagger walked back to our seats, I continued a quieter conversation with Paul.

"Is this putting Stacie right in the middle of it?" I whispered.

"We have her with motive, we have her with access to the victim. Mayor CJ didn't have her cell phone that night, but it was pinging off at the location of the lake cottage.

Which means Stacie had the mayor's cell phone with her.

Although we still need more evidence to get her on the murder of Hawk.

Otherwise, we can only arrest her for the murder of Chelsey and also for planting evidence. I'd like to get her on everything she did to you."

"Paul, as long as we get her for Chelsey's murder, she's going away.

If you can't find evidence of the sabotage on me, I can live with it, this community needs to be safe again."

"Ok, but I'm not giving up."

Suddenly, from behind the office door, the mayor appeared with her lawyer.

"I guess thanks are in order to Jagger."

Mayor CJ walked over to Jagger and shook his hand.

"Thank you, young man, for your courage to come forward with your eyewitness account, and that video, it has helped me more than you know.

Of course, a hero of the city, you're one of our lifeguards, good work, son."

Mayor CJ proudly acknowledged Jagger, as he stood in the lobby wearing his lifeguard uniform, red board shorts, and white t-shirt with the Rancho Niguel logo, and his regulation red windbreaker with the city logo on the front.

"You're welcome, Ms. Mayor, thank you."

After which, she turned to me.

"Nikki, may I have a word with you?"

"Of course."

We were out of earshot of the others, so we walked to the end of the lobby.

Mayor CJ looked tired but still upbeat in her grey pantsuit and her Gidget flip in caramel highlights.

"Nikki, I need you to help me."

Chapter 23

Four Heads Are Better Than One

Sara and Jagger went home for the evening, and I stayed behind to hash out a plan with the mayor and the police.

It was now later in the evening, and we were nowhere near a way to take down Stacie Mc. Daniels!

Mayor CJ was tired of Stacie and her outbursts. She had countless moments of embarrassment, and she had suspected her of some form of sabotage, but she had no evidence of it, just her own intuition.

Paul, Craig, and I sat in the boardroom at the police department, trying to put some kind of operation in motion.

"We need to find a way to catch her or to find evidence of her methods she used on us." Paul said.

"Truthfully, I've searched her desk, and I am sorry to say I haven't found anything; it's like there is no trail to follow.

Marge has been watching her, and that's how we managed to find out she was giving me pills."

The Mayor confided.

"She did the same thing to me, let me guess barbiturates."

"Yes, she did that to you, too, Paul."

Mayor CJ found it amusing.

"Yes!" He replied, embarrassed to admit to.

"She's hiding the evidence somewhere, I know it, but we just haven't found it.

I thought that maybe she was using the lake cottage to keep her plans." Paul remarked.

"I think we should still get a warrant for her home and do a search." Craig offered.

"No, we have to hit her by surprise; she can't know that we are on to her, or she'll just bolt.

Right now, she thinks she won, she believes that the Mayor will go down and that I'm going to marry her!"

Paul said.

Mayor CJ made a sour face.

"Oh my God, seriously, how did you get roped into that?"

"She believes I'm under her hypnosis."

"Oh, yeah, you're right."

Mayor CJ realized and agreed with Paul.

"What if we set her up, you know, like a sting operation?"

I suggested.

Everyone thought this over.

"What do you have in mind?"

Craig asked

"Well, what do you all think of this?"

Chapter 24

Fish Bait

There were only two things that would draw out Stacie McDaniels.

1. Paul

2. The Mayors position

I had turned this over in my head for a few minutes before I told everyone about my plan to catch Stacie.

According to our rules and regulations for mayoral duties, the mayor had the right to put an interim individual in her place should she be inclined due to illness, death, or legal disputes.

My plan was simple: I had to take everything of value away from Stacie.

We also hashed out the second part of my plan, I had to marry Paul in a very public ceremony.

The next morning, we put the plan in motion.

The mayor called a press conference to be held at the end of the boardwalk, where we sang earlier last week, to announce my interim position as Mayor of Rancho Niguel.

I had put in a call to Sara and Jagger last night and asked them not to spread any information yet about Jagger exonerating the mayor.

I told them they were part of a covert operation, and not even Matt was to know what was happening.

"Sara, there will be some events put in motion that we are doing to catch a killer. Don't be upset, and please keep your brother calm." This was all I told her as I swore her to secrecy!

She said she understood and she would fully cooperate in this mission.

Next, I planned my wardrobe, a navy suit with an aqua silk sleeveless blouse and strappy heels completed my new Mayor of the City ensemble.

The press conference began at 9 am Mayor CJ and Stacie were seated behind a podium with a microphone.

The press was here. Newspaper reporters, local TV news reporters, some small bloggers, and podcasters as well.

Stacie sat next to the Mayor, not knowing what was happening. The Mayor had told her that she had an announcement to make. I was standing off to the side of the press, awaiting my cue.

"Ladies and gentlemen, let's get started now."

Mayor CJ took the mic and began her speech.

"I am proud to be your Mayor here in Rancho Niguel and to have the privilege to lead a fine community of gracious residents, employees, kids, business owners, and many others.

I have been at this post for a year and 1/2 now, and I have enjoyed every minute of it.

So at this time, it saddens me to come to this decision, but with my legal challenges at this time, I need to focus on my defense."

Everyone here knew she had been called in for questioning, and this morning, the PD (Paul and Craig) had confirmed she was a person of interest in the murder of Chelsey Hall.

I watched Stacie sit up straighter and smile at the audience in front of her. I knew what she was thinking; she thought she had this position in the bag, and one of her ambitions would be coming true. Wrong!

Little did Stacie know she was about to get played!

"I'd like to hand off my mayoral duties to a woman who I know will shine in this position.

She's a lady of intelligence, a lady of fine moral character, and a fine community leader.

I am counting on her experience and fortitude to lead our beautiful city until I can come back to my post and fulfill my duties.

I'd like to introduce none other than the beautiful and talented woman." I saw Stacie smile brightly, and although she was just about to stand up to take her post, her smile suddenly faded and turned to horror when she heard Mayor CJ say,

"Ms. Nikki Rodriguez."

There were cheers and a lot of clapping.

My friends, the mystery investigation group, were here in the audience as well.

Matt, Sara, Martin, Jessica, Oliver, Tito, Daisy, Roxy, Mrs. Green, Betty Jean, Lisa, Marge, and Emily from the city hub station.

I walked to the microphone and accepted my honor.

"Thank you, Mayor CJ, I will do the city proud and do my best to fulfill these responsibilities."

We shook hands, and she passed me a makeshift gavel with the words Mayor engraved on the prop.

The press took photos and a few questions, and from the corner of my eye, I saw Stacie, and she looked angry enough to kill someone. After my congratulations from friends and community members, the Mayor and I were ushered into her waiting limo in the parking lot next to the boardwalk entrance, and we drove off.

"Do you think they bought it?"

"Oh yeah, did you see the look on Stacie's face?"

"Yes, she's coming after you."

"Wait until she sees phase two."

I replied as the mayor, and I toasted our glasses with bourbon.

I had to act fast. After the Mayor dropped me off at home, I put phase two in motion. I sent out my e-invites (invitations via text message) to all of my friends. I included Matt and Sara.

 I hated to do it, but I had to make it look real.

I knew I was going to freak out a few of my friends; they would be wondering what was going on, but I couldn't let anyone know what we were up to; it had to go down this way.

I also turned off my phone for a few hours to keep from hearing the backlash I would be getting.

So here it is! It went something like this:

The pleasure of your company is requested

At the Rancho Santa Ariana Mansion and Estate

Tomorrow, Saturday, August 21

At the hour of 12 noon

At the lakefront garden for

The Nuptials of

Nicole Rodriguez

to

Paul Anderson

Reception to follow at the Mansion

Later that evening, I placed a call to Paul.

"Ok, I put phase two in motion. Have you told her?"

"I did, Nikki, we were in a public place, having dinner at the outdoor mall when I told her."

"What happened?"

"She threw her champagne in my face, then she yelled like a psycho, and then stormed off.

We have her right where we want her."

"Ok, it looks like we have everything in place."

"Nikki, I'm worried about you. I can't believe you talked me into letting you be fish bait to catch her."

"Don't worry, Paul, everything will work out."

Chapter 25

Mr. & Mrs.

It was a beautiful morning, the sunlight danced in through my white curtains.

 I yawned and stretched in bed, willing myself to get up and get ready for my covert operation.

Last night, Matt came by my place, I heard his truck come to a stop, and then came the loud pound on my door.

He wasn't happy, and by all means, I felt like a real jerk not being able to tell him this was all a sham, but I had to make it look real.

"Please tell me this is a bad dream and you are not going to marry Paul?"

"Paul and I had a long conversation, and we came to the conclusion that this was the best option for us."

"Nikki, think about what you're doing here, please."

He put his hands on my shoulders, bracing for my answer.

"Don't worry, Matt, everything will be fine, I know what I'm doing."

"Nikki, don't go through with this!"

He was serious, his face filled with concern and desperation, especially when he was faced with the reality that I would marry someone else. He was begging me to reconsider what I was going to do. And at that moment, I knew Matthew Stevens truly loved me.

"Matt, everything is going to be ok, trust me."

He dropped his hands on my shoulders, defeat on his sad face. Always the gentleman, he straightened his posture and did the right thing. He held my hand and wished me happiness.

"I wish you all the happiness in the world, Nikki."

He walked out of the condo and drove away. I felt like slugging myself in the gut. I closed the door and went to my room.

***

I had such a short time frame to put this together, but I managed to find a beautiful white dress from Macy's. It took me half an hour, and a size 8 later, I carried out my dress and stopped by the florist to pick up a bouquet of white peonies.

I went home and got ready; the mayor's limo was coming for me at 11 am. I curled my long, dark hair, put on my dress, and my royal blue satin high heels. My make-up was sun-kissed, and my hands were clammy. This was harder than I thought.

I arrived at the mansion ready to go, Paul was standing at the makeshift bridal arch that was set up out of a white metal with cascading ivy and white peonies.

The guest list had been very small, and now everyone was seated and dressed in semi-formal attire.

Roxy walked up to me first, ready with her bouquet and dressed in her short, chiffon blush-colored maid of honor dress.

"I still can't believe you're going through with this, but I know you don't do anything unless it's the right thing to do."

She stated sounding sure of my choice.

"Don't worry, Roxy, everything will be fine." I smiled.

"Ok." She winked at me and stood in front of me, and then the music began.

A violinist played Pachelbel's Canon in D major, and Roxy walked down the aisle, the lake lay in front of her, with glistening gems of sparkling reflections from the sunlight.

Next up was me.

The violinist played the wedding march, and I walked toward Paul. Every step I took, I thought if this was real, it was a good deal, Paul would make a wonderful husband, and I did have an immense love for him.

If the circumstances were different, I know I would be very happy at this moment, instead of the gut-wrenching that was in motion right now. Was it because I felt like I had betrayed Matt?

I looked ahead and saw Paul; he looked dashing in his tuxedo, and his bright green eyes were calm and content.

I walked down the aisle in my white strapless chiffon gown with my friends watching and filling the ten white padded chairs set out for my guests.

Mrs. Green, Martin, Oliver, Jessica, Tito, Daisy, Sara, Jagger, Chef Stark, and Kiana.

On Paul's side, most were cops, ok, all of them were cops.

Craig stood beside Paul as his best man.

The officiant, not a real one but a vice cop undercover was ready with a black leather-bound book of Moby Dick in his hand and a fake collar around his neck.

I reached the arch, and Paul and I stood side by side.

We both looked into each other's eyes, and the vice cop began his part.

"Friends and family, we are gathered today to celebrate these two in marriage.

Nikki and Paul have come here with their consent in matrimony.

Nikki, please repeat after me.

I take you, Paul, as my life partner, in sickness and in health, for better or worse, from this day forward and for all the days of my life."

I said my vows while holding hands with Paul.

"Paul, now repeat after me, I take you, Nikki, as my life partner, in sickness and in health, for better or worse, from this day forward and for all the days of my life."

Paul repeated his vows to me, with a small smile and warmth in his hands.

"Now for the rings." Craig and Roxy handed over two plain gold rings, Roxy smiled and kissed my cheek, and I handed her my bouquet.

"Paul place the ring on Nikki's finger and repeat after me. With this ring, I pledge my love."

The gold band slid on my finger, and next, I took Paul's ring.

"Nikki, repeat after me as you place the ring on Paul's finger, with this ring I pledge my love."

Paul smiled at me, and for a split second, it felt real.

I sensed his love for me, and my love for him.

If this wasn't a setup, I would swear that we were wholeheartedly committing to a marriage.

I wasn't scared and I wasn't afraid! I was actually happy.

It was not what I thought I would be feeling.

I was in complete calm, and it was almost a euphoric bliss.

"Now, if there are no objections here." The vice cop looked around the audience.

No one objected; everyone was smiling, Oliver had tears in his eyes, dabbing at the corners of them with a silk white handkerchief.

"I pronounce you man and wife, you may kiss the bride."

Paul laid a big kiss on me, and everyone cheered and clapped.

We were smiling along with our guests, and we were just about to walk down the aisle to end the ceremony when lo and behold, our guest of honor showed up.

Standing at the end of the aisle holding a gun to Matt's head, she stood there dressed in a pair of skinny jeans and a very low-cut t-shirt, exposing her goodies and heaving large breaths, making her demands!

"I'm putting a stop to this wedding, I OBJECT!"

She shouted.

She held her position, holding her gun.

Stacie McDaniels had snapped!

Chapter 26

It's Over

Stacie looked haggard and angry! She snapped her fingers around Matt's ear a few times, and he blinked, now realizing where he was. He made the connection that he had been hypnotized and brought here as Stacie's hostage.

"Don't even try to escape or I'll end you."

Stacie shouted out to Matt, knowing he was ready to bolt.

"I want a trade, Matt Stevens for Paul Anderson."

I turned to Paul with a look of horror on my face.

We had no idea she would take a hostage, but Stacie had a card hidden up her sleeve.

"Stacie, you are surrounded by RNPD officers. Don't do this, think carefully."

"Oh, I have Paul!" She smirked.

"Ok, Stacie, let's talk about this. I don't want you to hurt anyone."

She walked with Matt down the aisle, now just a few feet away from us.

Craig and the other officers had their guns out and now pointed them at Stacie.

177

Two officers took the remainder of the wedding guests away from the ceremony, and they waited safely behind the gates of the mansion.

At this point, Stacie McDaniels had lost everything. Her job, her man, her position, and soon her freedom.

Paul walked in front of me as a protective shield.

"Stacie, it's time to turn yourself in. You have committed two murders, one against Hawk McGuire and one against Chelsey Hall, you have committed attempted murder twice against Nikki, and you have committed various thefts and vandalism of public and private property. You are wanted on charges of blackmail, arson, extortion, fraud, and hypnosis on your victims, and that's not including the federal charges that the FBI is placing on you. It's over!" Paul shouted.

Stacie looked around.

"I didn't kill Hawk McGuire." She stated.

"We have a lot of evidence against you, Stacie. Give up now, this won't end well."

He pleaded with her, giving her the last of his moral sympathy.

Stacie put on an air of arrogance and confessed.

"You're right Paul, I tried to sabotage that bride of yours, I did try to kill her with a nail gun, and I did pour acid on her car, I tried to kill her with the blast at Kendles, it sucks that it didn't work! Yes, I did destroy the gym floor at the community center. I tried to take the Mayor's job because I am better at it than she is, and I did try to frame her for Chelsey's murder. I alerted the press last October about the vampire killer, and I told the press about the Russian gun runners, I did it all, Paul, because I wanted Nikki dead!"

She yelled, but continued her rant.

" All I wanted was you, Paul."

Stacie was crying, but still, she held a Glock to Matt's head.

"All I wanted was you, and Nikki was always getting in the way. Nikki is so talented, Nikki is so wonderful, Nikki this Nikki that! Everything revolved around her, so yes, I hate Nikki, and I tried to take her out of your life, and now, there's nothing left to fight for; she won! She is your wife now!"

Anger colored her face, her body tight and rigid with power and force, so that she held the upper hand at this point.

"Why did you kill Hawk?" I asked Stacie.

"I didn't kill Hawk; he and I had an understanding, he wasn't going to blab about Cliffside, and I wasn't going to tell that he paid off three of the city council members to vote in his favor."

"What about Chelsey Hall?"

"Oh that one, after Hawk died she came around telling me I had to pay her to keep my secret from getting out about Cliffside, I paid her once but it wasn't enough she got greedy and came and met me at the mansion but I told her I had the money at the lake cottage, so she followed me over there, we got into an argument over the amount and I reached for the knife in the kitchen and killed her." She said matter of fact and without remorse.

Just then, the FBI surrounded Stacie.

Paul walked closer to Stacie. He held his hand out to her and asked for the gun.

"Stacie, give me the gun, it's over!"

She looked around her, now seeing all of the cops and the Feds with their guns drawn on her.

"I want my trade!"

She pushed Matt forward.

"Ok, Stacie, we'll trade."

"Don't try anything, Paul!" Stacie yelled, holding the gun to Matt's head.

She kicked Matt in the shin, and when he dropped down to the floor, she put her gun to Paul's head.

Paul stayed in front of me, shielding me from Stacie's line of fire.

"Matt, stay down low."

Paul told him, but it was too late. Matt grabbed me by the waist and removed me from the line of fire.

"No!" Stacie yelled.

She turned the gun towards Nikki, but Paul was quick and he stopped her by overpowering her hands and head-butting her. The gun was in Paul's hand now, and Craig and the other officers dove in to handcuff her.

Paul disarmed the gun and gave it to a fellow officer who held a plastic evidence bag for it.

Matt and I were sitting on a padded white chair, catching our breath.

Paul came over to me and grabbed me up into a big hug.

"It's over, It's all over."

With tears running down my cheeks, I felt a complete wave of gratitude for the finality of all that had happened over the last year. Paul was right; it was all finally over.

Matt got up quietly and made his way down to the mansion.

"I have to go and talk to him." I told Paul after we parted.

"Sure,"

Agent Caleb Tores walked over to us.

"Nikki, you were right, all of this pulled her out to confess, nice job, Mrs. Anderson."

Caleb joked about Mrs. Part.

"You know it wasn't real, Caleb."

He high-fived me. "Good work, special agent Nikki."

He and Paul began to discuss the events, I went to go and speak with Matt.

"Matt."

I called out just before he walked past the police barricade.

He breathed out a large sigh as if he was bothered by me, but turned around to face me head-on.

"Nikki, you're married, and I'm going to accept that, ok, so just leave me alone!" He turned to walk away.

"Thank you for pulling me out of the way. Paul and I are not married! It was an undercover operation."

He turned around and walked back to me; the spark came back to his eyes.

"It was?" He asked, looking surprised!

He was speechless for a few seconds, and then he said.

"So none of this was real?"

"Nope, the officiant was a vice cop, not a pastor. The vows were fake, and so was everything else. We had to take everything away from Stacie to lure her out; we needed her to snap, so she would give herself up, and it worked. I'm just sorry she got you involved."

"That's why you didn't tell me last night, you needed to make it look real."

Matt put it all together, a small smile coming to the corners of his mouth.

"Yes, and I'm so sorry if this caused you any stress or anything else."

"I have to admit you guys did a good job of making it look real."

"Thanks, we worked hard on it, look, no one knew, not even Roxy, and she's my best friend.

The only ones who knew were the FBI, Craig, the mayor, Paul, and me." Matt smiled now,

"A covert operation, pretty good, should we tell the others now?"

Matt said, nodding in the direction of all of our friends waiting in front of the mansion.

"I have a catered meal waiting for everyone in there."

Craig came up to us,

"Matt, I'm going to need your statement about your abduction from Stacie. Do you have a few minutes?"

"Sure Craig."

"I'll meet you guys in there. Craig, tell the feds and the PD crew there is food inside if they want to eat; there is plenty for everyone."

"Hey, thanks, Nikki, I'm a little famished myself."

He patted his tight abs.

"I'll see you guys in a while."

I waved back.

"Hey Nikki, I forgot to tell you, you look beautiful."

Matt told me with a big smile.

I smiled, rolled my eyes, and walked to the mansion.

Chapter 27

When The Sun Goes Down

I looked at my friends waiting patiently behind the police barricade.

They looked shocked and relieved at the same time.

An RNPD police vehicle with Stacie in the back seat pulled away from the scene. I turned to my friends.

"Ok, if all of you will follow me to the reception, I had Kendle's cater a nice meal for us, and I'll explain everything."

Mrs. Green, Martin, Oliver, Jessica, Tito, Daisy, Sara, Jagger, Roxy, and Kiana followed me into the Rancho Santa Ariana Mansion for some food and some cocktails.

All of them were asking questions at the same time and were now talking over each other with excitement.

We took our seats at a long banquet table set with napkins and silverware.

I had a nice buffet set up and asked everyone to get a plate and then have a seat.

When everyone of them was seated, I sat at the head of the table and began.

"I know you are all wondering what happened!

The plan was to have me take everything away from Stacie to basically make her crack so she would confess.

Paul, Craig, Mayor CJ, and I made the necessary plans to have me become interim mayor and then invite you all to my wedding to Paul.

Once Stacie lost everything we knew, she would crash the wedding.

We went over the plan with agent Caleb for backup, and for the fact that they had federal charges pending on her allowed us to team up.

Paul and Craig got a warrant for her apartment, and we found her files behind the washer and dryer.

We also found a safe in the mayor's cottage with more files and notes from her deliberate hypnosis plan that she carried out on Paul and Mayor CJ.

A leather tote bag filled with her journal, the wire transfers, and all of the evidence from the takeover at Cliffside was there, too.

The only thing is we don't know where she moved the money, but I'm sure the feds will find it.

She's going down for everything that she has done."

Everyone was speechless with surprise and curiosity.

"Also, you should know that Paul and I aren't married, the officiant is a vice cop, he was undercover too.

I'm sorry, guys, but we had to make it look real; we couldn't risk that someone would slip up that it was fake."

I told them. Everyone shook their heads in agreement that they understood the secrecy behind the whole operation.

The buffet of fresh king salmon, shrimp scampi, scallops, filet mignon steaks, mashed potatoes, a summer salad, and sautéed green beans was calming to the nerves, and my guests were relaxing a bit more.

Everyone was talking and giving their opinion on what happened today.

The cocktails didn't hurt either. Craig, Matt, and Paul entered the banquet room in the mansion.

They went to the buffet and then brought their plates to the table. It seemed like a nice chat they were having, and for once, Paul and Matt were civilized and not trying to fight with one another.

"I will say this, you guys pulled together one heck of a wedding, even though it wasn't real. Roxy commented.

"I'll second that." Paul raised his beer to it.

"Well, here is to the two of you, congratulations on your fake marriage in the apprehension of a murderer. Here's to Mr. and Mrs. Not married."

We all held up our glasses and cheered to capture a killer.

More of the law enforcement officers came in for a meal, some RNPD, and some FBI agents.

Caleb had some food but stated he and his team couldn't stay long, they had to be out on a plane in a few hours.

The talk continued with everyone asking Craig and Paul about the crimes that Stacie committed.

We were on coffee and dessert when Roxy told Paul.

" I'm glad that I'm not in your crosshairs as a suspect anymore."

Roxy addressed her comment to Craig and Paul.

"Yes, we are too!" They replied.

"I have a question: why did Stacie cop to everything but killing Hawk?"

Tito asked.

"Stacie was desperate; she probably thought if she didn't admit it, then she wouldn't be charged with it, who knows?"

Craig finished saying.

"That is strange, to admit to all of the other crimes and not to killing Hawk?"

Mrs. Green chimed in.

I thought this over too; she insisted that she didn't kill Hawk.

Then who did?

The more I thought about it, the more I realized that Hawk's killer wasn't Stacie; Hawk's killer was someone we missed.

Chapter 27

A Crazy Plea

The arrest of Stacie Mc. Daniels was all over the news.

Every Chanel had a story on her crimes over the last five years.

Our little town was once again flooded with reporters and cameras,

all hoping to get the story of a lifetime.

Stacie was advised by her lawyer not to speak with any reporters,

but as stubborn as she is, she chose to speak to Flame Phillips.

My old pal, who helped me with a case back in October, Flame,

got his exclusive with the vampire killer and then went national.

He was hired on by a big news conglomerate in New York City.

Flame was a former resident here, and Stacie knew him.

She knew that Flame was very familiar with all of the players in

the story, and she claimed to want pure authenticity from a former

local. The day after she was arrested, she was arraigned for her

crimes here in Rancho Niguel, then she was whisked off to Los

Angeles to face federal charges for the crimes at Cliffside.

Before she left for L.A., Flame sat down with her for a one-on-one exclusive interview.

Roxy and I watched it on TV while having popcorn, wine, and some charcuterie.

"Can you believe she's giving an interview this soon?"

"I know Roxy, it's crazy her lawyer told her to stay quiet, this could really bite her in the butt!"

At 7 pm, we and most of Rancho Niguel and the rest of the country tuned in to watch.

Stacie was in a denim blue jumpsuit with her dark hair curled and only lip gloss on. She sat with confidence and claimed her innocence, she seemed completely unaware of the serious nature of her alleged crimes.

"What would you like to tell everyone that's watching?"

Flame asked her.

"Well, I would just like to say that I am innocent of all the crimes that I am charged with. This is nothing more than an attempt from Nikki Rodriguez to get me."

"What do you mean, to get you? Why would she want to do that?"

Flame asked her, patiently waiting for her response.

"Nikki Rodriguez has been jealous of me the whole time I have been in Rancho Niguel. She stole my man, she stole my rightful

place to be interim mayor, and she has continued to spread lies to everyone about me trying to sabotage her. She is nothing but a liar!"

"Witnesses at the scene on Saturday at the nuptials of Nikki Rodriguez and Paul Anderson say they heard you confess to all of the crimes, along with officers and FBI agents.

What do you say about that confession?"

"I was under extreme duress, Flame. I was in so much pain that I would have said anything to get some help."

Flame looked very surprised by her reaction; his eyebrows rose, and he went to the next question.

"Ms. McDaniels, the evidence against you is very strong, your crimes began long before you met Ms. Rodriguez. I'm talking about Cliff Side. What do you have to say about those crimes?"

"Flame, I'm telling you the people from Cliff Side are just out to get me. I did nothing wrong."

"There are lawsuits against Hawk McGuire's company and also against you. How can that be another group of people out to get you? You have to see that you had a part in this."

"Flame, I am the victim here. I did nothing but provide counseling services to the folks at Cliff Side, I was a right hand to the mayor of Rancho Niguel, I am the one being railroaded."

She smiled several times during her interview, trying to capture the camera and proceeding to name herself as the victim of the crimes she committed.

Flame wrapped up his interview with Stacie, then she was led back to her cell, and Flame continued with the rest of his reporting.

"Stacie McDaniel's lawyer is here with us. What happens next for her?" Flame asked Stacie's lawyer.

"Next, Ms. McDaniels will have a psych evaluation to decide if she is competent for the case."

"Well, this is a twist. Why wouldn't she be competent?"

"I can't say anymore, Mr. Phillips."

With that, Flame wrapped up his interview.

"Well folks you heard it here, it looks like the defense is planning on an insanity plea, just a guess but we will see what happens, next week, I will be reporting on this case for the duration of the outcome, thank you for watching tonight, I'm Flame Phillips reporting from the city jail in Rancho Niguel, California."

I turned off the tube and turned to Roxy.

"I guess this is it, she wants to plead insanity."

"No way, she knew exactly what she was doing, but you're right, she knows how to play the game and she's going to end up in a psychiatric hospital."

"Maybe not, the doctors will know she is playing them right?" Roxy asked.

"Nope, I don't think they will have a clue."

Chapter 28

Lazy On The Lake

The last few days of August, I spent relaxing. The temperature climbed to 98 degrees, and everyone was out on the lake.

The paperwork was wrapped up on Stacie McDaniels at the department, but the FBI was still adding to her case.

I sent Agent Caleb a bottle of the best quality whiskey I could get my hands on, and some cigars from Cuba, I mean Florida, Little Havana (shhh, don't tell! I know they are illegal).

Paul had clued me in to Caleb's favorite things, and this was a simple thank you for all of his help.

Paul and I kept our gold bands as a memento of the sting operation we did to capture Stacie.

I put mine in my jewelry box, and occasionally, I put it on just for educational merit to scientifically see if it feels rational.

Ok, ok, I put it on and think to myself it's not so bad, marriage, love, the house in the suburbs, some really cute kids, and PTA meetings, sitting on the school board, attending sports events, or school plays.

I began to see some of it, and it didn't feel bad at all.

I remembered the feeling of seeing Paul at the end of the aisle, and I romanticized that if it *had* been real, well, I felt happy at that moment, and all of the nervous knots were gone.

I saw Paul, and he made everything around us feel like pure happiness.

I wasn't worried or scared, I just felt like a woman in love and ready for her next adventure.

My wedding dress, which I donated to the church's pancake breakfast and silent auction, went very well.

Because of the backstory on it and the fact that now, apparently, I'm a local celebrity, it brought in $4000.00 for St. Mark's. Catholic Church. Father Reilly was glowing with delight.

The money would provide funds for the Sisters of Rancho Niguel, the place where the nuns reside. They needed some upgrades on their housing, plumbing, and electrical systems on the property.

Of course, I donated some funds from Kendle's along with new living room and bedroom furniture, bedding, and some new towels, robes, and slippers.

Mother Superior and the nuns were grateful and sent me a very sweet thank-you note and a prayer dedication to keep me safe amidst my sleuthing.

I don't get into that much trouble, do I?

Matt was more than understanding about the fake wedding. He asked me to come along with him on his boat the following Sunday, but I told him I already had plans.

Paul had asked me to save Sunday for a lake day, he said I wouldn't be disappointed.

On Sunday morning, he arrived at 9 am, and he brought some pastries and two beach break breakfasts from Stella's Coffee Shop. We sat down at the dining table and feasted on eggs Benedict with fresh crab and sea salt home potatoes, thick-cut bacon, and fresh fruit.

"This looks fabulous, you can bring me breakfast any day of the week."

I told him taking a bite of Hollandaise sauce and that scrumptious crab meat with a poached egg.

He smiled, "Anything for Mrs. Anderson." He replied, making a light joke.

"I laughed and replied, "Oh my gosh, it's never going to end, is it?"

"I don't think it sounds too bad, does it?"

He smiled with those fabulous green pools of Caribbean ocean eyes.

"So what is it that we are doing the rest of the day?"

I changed the subject fast.

"Finish up, and then we'll go. I have a day on the lake for the two of us. Don't forget to wear a swimsuit under your clothes."

After breakfast, we drove down to the lake. It was early, so there weren't many people out just yet, and the sun was already bursting with heat.

We walked to the marina, and Paul led me to a slip with a white and red boat.

"Is this yours?"

"Yes, I just bought it. It's a used boat, but it's in immaculate condition. The guy I bought it from is moving to Vermont for work, and he needed to sell it to buy a house.

Wait until you see the surprise I have for you."

I think maybe this is where Paul put the $8500 from the trip. I didn't mind it was, after all, a gift.

The boat was a Cobalt, or so the name said in silver block lettering, stainless steel on the side of the stern.

Along with the word SURF painted on the stern of the boat and the letters R6 on the side by the name Cobalt.

The seats were dark grey and white with red thread trim.

Fancy! The seating area held a cutty cab in the bow section and then the two seats in the middle of the boat, a passenger seat and the driver's seat, then behind the passenger seat was a U-shaped seating area, and then behind it was a bench seat at the stern.

In front of the passenger seat, a small door opened to a small head with a few steps down into the hull of the boat.

We got in, and I set my beach bag in one of the bench seats to keep it from getting wet.

Paul started the engine and put on some tunes, and we were speeding off to the tune of "Jamming" by Bob Marley.

After a few turns around, we slowed and coasted off into a small clearing.

"Ok, now here is the surprise, this boat has a unique feature, we can surf behind it." He claimed with so much excitement.

"What, no way how?"

I asked him, not seeing how it was possible.

We anchored for a few minutes and set up for our surfing boards.

"Put on a life vest."

Paul handed me a red and grey life vest that I put on over my red tankini.

He took a small surfboard that was hanging on the side of the rails that held up an awning or shade over the top of the boat.

He placed the board in the water.

"Go ahead, jump on."

I followed his instructions to get on the board like I would on a regular surfboard.

I stood up on the board, and he handed me a water ski line.

I held the line and put my hands on the plastic part, holding on to it as if I were going to water ski.

He gave me some instructions and safety tips, and then I told him I was ready to try it.

He went back to start the boat and told me to surf ski until I felt comfortable enough to let go of the line.

I took a deep breath and told myself here we go!

Paul pulled the anchor and then started the engine back up.

He pressed a few buttons on the screen on the driver's dashboard to start the surf option.

The next thing I knew, a part of the stern opened to one side and began creating a wave in the lake water.

It moved side to side, creating small wake waves.

Paul put a little speed on, and I was surfing the waves side to side, gliding back and forth.

The song changed to "Surfin' USA" by The Beach Boys.

I was getting comfortable with the movement and felt confident enough to let go of the line.

I spent the next fifteen minutes surfing around the lake, my adrenaline going, and my handiwork from my surfing going to play.

I had a blast! Swishing and zig-zagging and moving with waves. It was unreal! This was the next best thing if we couldn't get out on the ocean. Lake surfing was awesome!

Paul pulled into a small cove, and I changed places with him after he gave me a crash course on how to drive the boat.

He took his turn surfing and swishing on the lake in the waves.

He looked so pro, surfing to the tune of "Misirlou," an instrumental song by the Beach Boys.

We had a few boaters look at us and give us the thumbs up.

"That's so cool, Lake surfing."

That was what one fellow boater shouted out to us.

A few other boaters clapped and pointed to us as if saying;

"You're the man, bro!"

We took a few more turns surfing and then, by 2 pm, decided on having some lunch.

"I'm starving, are you?" Paul asked, coming back onto the stern of the boat.

"Definitely I'm starving too."

Paul dried off with a beach towel and then went to the head to wash his hands. After that, he went to the cooler that was built into the boat.

He brought out two sub sandwiches and two Cokes.

I pulled out a bag of Doritos chips and some napkins from one of the bench seats' storage areas.

The music changed to "Red Red Wine" by UB40, an 80s classic.

"Were those waves wild?" Paul asked, but rather made more of a statement.

Then he took a bite of his sub sandwich.

"It was amazing, I never knew surfing like that was possible."

I replied, then took a drink of Coke.

"So tell me what made you buy a boat?"

The music changed to "It's Five O'Clock Somewhere."

By Alan Jackson and Jimmy Buffett.

He wiped his mouth and then said;

"I guess I spent a lot of time this summer out on lake patrol, and then I saw an ad on social media about boat surfing, and then I looked around for someone selling a boat, and I was lucky enough to find one.

I jumped at the chance to buy it from that dude I was telling you about, the one who owned this boat.

I guess it was the right one for me."

"That's true, I believe, when something is meant to be, everything else will just fall in line."

"Yeah." He replied.

I didn't want to bring her up, but I wanted to know how Paul was doing with all of the Stacie hype, the arrest, the interview, and so forth.

"Hey, how are you doing with the case?" I asked him.

He finished his sip of Coke and thought first, then he replied.

"For a few days, I had to turn it off!

I bought the boat and took it out around the lake to think and find some peace. It gave me a new outlook.

Nikki, I'm looking for it now: happiness, a relationship with commitment.

After we had the mock wedding, it got me thinking, it's not so bad, you know.

I thought about if it had been a real wedding, coming home to you at the end of my day, sharing a lifetime with you.

The kids, the vacations, family holidays, and I thought it seemed like it could be an adventure that I'm ready for."

"Well, this is quite an epiphany you had."

"Yeah, talk about insight, right?"

"So where do you go from here?"

"I'd like to get back together, Nikki."

Paul wasn't the only one who wanted to get back together; Matt had expressed this too, and now, once again, I was in a love triangle.

I had to choose one soon, before things got complicated again.

I didn't want a repeat of Valentine's Day.

"Let me think about this, ok?"

"OK, whenever you're ready. Let's take it slow."

He held my hand, reassuring me of his support.

He had gotten bitten by the marriage bug, too, just like Matt.

Oh no, what next?

Chapter 29

Wipe Out

It was Monday, and today the final vote was scheduled to take place on the future of the Rancho Santa Arianna Mansion and Estate.

Roxy and I arrived early and selected a row of seats for us and Dr. Neil Forbes president of the Historical Society, Rhonda Timbers executive assistant of the Preservation Society, and the one who was bullied by Stacie when she tossed her purse off the seat the last time we all met for the vote on the mansion.

As well as a few of the members of the mystery investigation group, Mrs. Green, Martin, Oliver, and Matt.

When noon rolled around, the room was standing room only, and many local members of the community came out to lend support for the old girl.

The signs read SAVE THE HISTORICAL GAL, AND DON'T DESTROY OUR HISTORY.

The city council sat down in front of a large audience, with Mayor CJ in the middle of them, standing at the podium.

"Ladies and Gentlemen, it's time to begin our meeting. If I can have everyone's attention, we will begin."

She said now with her lighter caramel flip, and wearing a light aqua sundress with a white blazer.

We all recited the Pledge of Allegiance, and then Marge took the minutes and read the agenda for today's meeting.

Dressed in her bright fuchsia sundress and her painted white mock pearls and white plastic cuff bracelet, she read on with her light blue vintage spectacles dangling from a delicate gold chain.

"On the agenda, today will be the final decision to preserve or to remove the Rancho Santa Ariana Mansion and Estate.

The floor recognizes Mayor CJ Groves."

Marge sat down now, and Mayor CJ spoke again.

"Today we are here to have a historic vote, and I won't waste time; I will get right down to it."

We were on pins and needles, Roxy and I; she was biting her red lip and slowly breathing in and out.

Her hands rested on her lap amidst the black a-line dress she wore, modest and cute with her fabulous bleached blonde due in a French twist. I sat up and kept my stare towards the sitting group of individuals that made up the city council.

Roger Penny, Pamela Jayapel, Rose Metcalf, and Jet Montrose. There they sat looking innocent and studious, I knew that three out of the four of them had been bribed, the thing was that we didn't know which ones.

Paul had begun an investigation into them, but it would take a few weeks to get through the background on them, and he needed to subpoena the bank records.

I rubbed my hands on the hem of my navy blue A-line summer dress, my hair hanging in a low bun to cool my neck from the intense heat outside.

I opted for simple heels in a barely nude color and a simple gold necklace with a loop pendant.

We took this vote very seriously, and we wanted our attire to reflect our dedication to professionalism.

 "For the vote to keep the Rancho Santa Ariana Mansion and Estate, please say I". The mayor asked.

Two "I's" were recorded by Rose Metcalf and Jet Montrose. Next were the No's by Roger Penny and Pamela Jayapal.

We were in a tie two against two, and now the Mayor's vote would give us the final vote.

She cozied back to the microphone and smiled a large, bleached white teeth grin with enthusiasm, and she said;

"As Mayor of this fine city, I vote to keep the mansion."

She wailed triumphantly and raised her hands for the win for the community.

Everyone in the room broke out in cheers, high fives, and a few hallelujahs. I looked at Roxy, and we hugged and smiled and became giddy with happiness.

Rhonda and Dr. Forbes high-fived and clapped.

Our row, along with everyone else, cheered.

"We saved the mansion, we saved her!"

"Now, ladies and gentlemen, the meeting is adjourned!"

Mayor CJ slammed her gavel, and it was done.

The Rancho Santa Ariana Mansion and Estate was saved from demolition; it would always stand tall and be a precious part of Rancho Niguel.

After the meeting broke up, many went outside with the protesters to cheer and add the victory on social media.

I felt great inside knowing that all of this would be preserved.

"Nikki, let's go outside and celebrate." Mrs. Green said.

"It's much needed." I replied.

I was following my friends toward the exit when

Rose Metcalf, one of the city council members, came to me.

"Nikki, can I have a word with you for just a few minutes?"

"Sure."

I looked at my friends and told them I would be right out.

We waited until the crowd of people left the room, and Rose led

me to the sitting room across from the auditorium.

"Please have a seat, Nikki."

I sat on the plush ivory sofa and crossed my legs.

Rose walked to the small liquor cart in the room, holding a pitcher

of water.

"Would you like a glass of cold water?"

She asked me, already pouring one for herself.

"Yes, that would be lovely, thank you."

She put ice in the glass from the ice bucket sitting on the cart,

filled the glass with a crystal pitcher of water, and handed it to me.

"Well, you're probably wondering why I asked to speak with you."

"Yes, is everything ok?" I asked.

She smiled.

"I wanted to thank you, Nikki, from the bottom of my heart.

Thank you for catching that horrid woman, Stacie McDaniels."

"You're welcome, I was happy to do it."

"I know. I am aware of your history; she completely sabotaged

you, and she tried to kill you.

You had all of the means in the world to go after her and seek

justice. I applaud you."

She placed her hand to her heart as if to say I understand.

Then she continued.

"But you see, I, too, have something in common with you."

She was sitting across from me now on the small loveseat in ivory,

her tall stature dressed in dark slacks and a yellow blouse flattering

her larger figure.

Her blond hair down to her shoulders curled at the bottom and put

half to one side. She dressed sharply, I'd give her that, she had a

certain elegance and mature stature to her.

"I was a victim of Stacie McDaniels, too!"

She admitted.

I was taken aback by her testimony.

"Did she try to blackmail you, too?"

"No, it was a bit different for me. You see, Nikki, Hawk McGuire,

and Stacie McDaniels robbed my mother of her inheritance.

Just a quick recap for you, my father was very wealthy, with family

money, and when he married my mother, she was poor, but he

loved her very much, and when he died, he left her very secure.

But she was getting on in age, and putting her in a facility was for her protection.

I was working in Boston, my brother was in Texas, and we were far away from her.

I had my inheritance from my father, he had split it two ways between my brother and me, and it was a very nice inheritance, and I did very well.

Then one day, when I went to visit my mother at Cliffside, she told me what was going on.

I acted on her behalf and looked into her banking and realized she had been robbed of all of her money.

She was broke! It was all gone!

So I moved out here to California, and my mother lived with me until she passed on a year later.

She was never the same; she blamed herself for not having better judgment of character, and she suffered from the guilt of the whole situation.

I filed a lawsuit against Hawks Company, and I filed a civil lawsuit against Stacie McDaniels.

So you can imagine my surprise when I found out that in my city, Hawk McGuire was going to do his dirty work again."

My mouth had dropped open, and in all of the few minutes it took to tell her story, I knew who killed Hawk McGuire!

She stood up with her glass of water and walked around the room, continuing her story, while I sipped my glass of ice water.

"He came to me, he paid me to change the vote in his favor, oh, he wanted this property badly.

I could see the greed on his face, that loathsome loser. The funny thing is that he didn't even have a clue who he was paying.

I took his money, all ten grand that he offered.

I know it wasn't much, but it was the satisfaction I got when I told him I needed more money.

You see, I wanted to make him go broke; I wanted him to feel the humility of someone robbing him blind.

So I met up with him a few more times, and a few more times he paid a bigger amount of money. $10k turned into to $100k and then $200k.

He knew the value of the property would be in the hundred million range; he was going to sell each home for $ 1.7-2 million each.

He was looking to make about 48 million dollars.

Then I told him that night who I was. We met at the new pier right underneath it, so no one would see us.

I told him if he paid back the money he stole from my mother, then I would drop my lawsuit against him, and he would never hear from me again. Honestly, I was asking him for five million dollars, that's what he had taken from her, and I wanted it back! The greed from him came out, and he told me to stuff it.

The look on his narcissistic face was cagey, and he was nothing but a thug in a suit.

He turned his back on me, and then he began to walk away, and he said, "You're a sucker just like your mother."

At that moment, I had so much rage! Something inside of me broke! I had just come from a drumming class with Roxy. Drums were something I always wanted to learn, so I had been taking classes at the community center, and I had my drumsticks in my bag. I pulled one out, and I stabbed him!"

She admitted it right out in the open, clear and precise, she told me how she killed Hawk, the look on her face calm and stable, she had no second thoughts about it, just as casual as if she had just killed a bug in her living room.

As I was listening to her story, I felt tired, the image of her was fading, and the light in the room was dimming.

The next thing she said sounded muffled, but I made it out.

"Nikki, I slipped you a sleeping pill. Don't worry, I'm not going to hurt you. I just need time to get away. I think we could have been great friends, and I am truly glad you kicked Stacie's butt.

That woman needed it!"

She smiled, then looked at her diamond-studded watch and said.

"I hate to leave, but I have to be somewhere.

Your friends will find you briefly."

She put a black and gold floral silk scarf over her hair and tied it around under her chin like the gals in the 1940s did.

Then she put on a pair of large, dark Chanel sunglasses and...

I wiped out!

Chapter 30

Escape

I woke up hours later, lying in my bed at home. The room was dark, and when I looked over at my nightstand, the small silver clock with Roman numerals read 8:25.

I had to get up; I felt like I had slept for days.

I went to my bathroom sink to brush my teeth and comb out my hair. I put on a pair of shorts and a T-shirt and opened my bedroom door.

I heard plenty of chatting, and my microwave was heating some popcorn.

"Nikki, finally, you're up." Mrs Green said while checking my temperature with her hand on my forehead.

"Ok, no temp, and you seem fine, come and sit down."

She led me to the sofa where Roxy, Matt, Paul, Jessica, Martin, Oliver, Marge, Kiana, Craig, Tito, Daisy, Sara, Jagger, and Flame sat scattered about the living room.

"She's back." Craig chimed in.

I sat down, and someone handed me a glass of iced tea.

"Are you hungry? We have some food from Del La Sol, your favorite?" Jessica asked.

"Oh, yeah, I'm starving."

Sara went to fix me a plate of food.

"So are you up to telling us what happened?" Paul asked me.

"Yeah, it was Rose Metcalf, she killed Hawk McGuire!"

Sara came back with a plate of taquitos and guacamole, with a big spoonful of rice and chips, and salsa.

"Thank you."

"No prob, now talk. Tell us what happened." Sara asked enthusiastically.

I retold the story that Rose told me about how she accepted the payouts from Hawk as getting revenge for her late mother and how she went into a rage when Hawk told her about being a sucker just like her mother.

I gave Craig, Paul, and everyone else the whole story, and now my audience was speechless.

Craig and Flame had been taking notes, and then Craig mentioned giving a formal statement later on.

"Wow, so she killed Hawk?" Martin asked.

"I never figured her for the type to kill; she took my drumming classes, and I thought she was a nice woman."

Roxy stated feeling like she had missed something.

Paul and Craig made some quick calls and went to the kitchen to converse with one another.

"But Nikki, just wondering why did she tell you all of this?" Daisy asked.

"I don't know, I guess she needed to get it off her chest, maybe she felt that she could confide in me, she did say she wasn't trying to hurt me, but that she just needed to buy some time."

"I think she needed to tell because she knew she was leaving town." Oliver said, giving his opinion.

After I finished my dinner, we all discussed the case, Paul and Craig had to leave, and they mentioned doing some investigation on Rose.

I walked them to the door, and Craig and Kiana left. He told Paul he wanted to walk Kiana home, but that he would meet him later at the station.

"Are you going to arrest Rose Metcalf?"

I asked Paul.

"We called for officers to go to her place, and they said it was empty; she's gone. Her convertible black Mercedes was found at the border of Tijuana, Mexico."

"What!"

"Yeah, she had an eight-hour start on us.

Hey, don't mention it yet to the others, we are still investigating."

"Ok, my lips are sealed."

"I'll check on you tomorrow, maybe breakfast around 10 am?"

"Sure."

"I'll see ya."

"Oh yeah, you do like Pina Coladas, right? Do you love to dance in the rain?"

"Are you taking out a personal ad or something?"

"Maybe," He replied with a small smile.

"Yes, but you have to have a brain, that's a deal breaker!"

I replied. He laughed a little.

"Ok, and maybe we can have a little escape."

"I think I can arrange that."

 I said, leaning against the front door.

"You know, there is a song similar to what you are saying."

"Oh yeah, I love that song, it's called "Escape" by Rupert Holmes.

My mom bought that album, I'm pretty familiar with it."

"I'm impressed, Paul." I teased.

 "I know what you're thinking, and I guess my humor seems a little morbid right now, talking about getting together. I just wanted to see you smile, Nikki."

"Thank you, and I'll see you tomorrow."

"Ok, tomorrow." He said.

I closed the door and went back to my guests...

The next day, Paul dropped by at 10 am just like he said he would.

He brought French toast and thick-cut bacon from Stella's Coffee Shop.

"Hi, have you slept?"

I asked him while getting the food out of the to-go boxes.

I placed some French press coffee in front of him.

"I'm fine, I had about six hours, that's good for me.

I have some news. For one thing, two of the city council members have been charged with taking a bribe: Pamela Jayapal and Roger Penny. They will most likely serve a year, but they will be removed from the city council.

Plus, I also have news on Rose Metcalf."

We sat down and ate and discussed what happened to Rose Metcalf.

"So what happened to Rose? Did you guys find her yet?"

"No, Rose Metcalf, also known as Rose De Boise, her maiden name, which is why Hawk had no idea who she was.

Let's just say that Rose drove off into the sunset.

We found her car at the border, like I told you, then the trail gets cold. She has no accounts here in the States, so everything is most likely overseas.

We did get a wire from the Mexican Federales that she entered Tijuana and from there she chartered a flight to who knows where. They didn't know, and most likely she's in a country with no extradition laws."

"She got her revenge and free and clear she escaped ..."

Today is August 30, and it's my birthday!

I didn't have any plans for today except for the fact that Roxy and Jessica were taking me to lunch and then to get mani-pedis at our favorite salon.

Daisy and Tito offered to take my night shift today so I could enjoy my birthday and not have to work.

I told them it's Sunday and we are, of course, busy, and I will be in, but later, around 6 pm.

They didn't argue but just said "No problem, boss."

The ladies picked me up at noon, and we went to Tokyo Sky, a Japanese restaurant where they cook and entertain you at your table.

We sat on soft, black, cushioned seats with rice paper walls and decorations of cherry blossom trees.

The lobby had suits of samurai lined up that you could take selfies with, and the water lily pond in the middle of the restaurant served as a backdrop for the elegance of the atmosphere.

After that, the ladies and I got pampered with spa mani-pedis. I chose a nice bright fuchsia for my toes and a French manicure for my hands.

The ladies dropped me back at home by 3:30 pm, and I took an hour nap on the patio.

By 5 pm, I got up and showered, and dressed for my shift at work. The band took the night off, so this evening was just the house music.

I decided on a nice royal blue a-line dress, sleeveless but with a nice conservative, slight plunge neckline, no boob showing, but ever so slightly a bit of cleavage that lends to the elegant mystery of being a woman.

When I arrived at the back kitchen entrance, my cooks and chefs were busy sautéing, frying, tossing, and seasoning on the stoves and around the counters.

"Hello, everyone."

They said hi and went back to their work.

Chef Stark came to my side right away, "Nikki, I need your attention in the banquet room. We had a slight issue with the chandelier."

He looked worried. "Oh no, what now!"

I asked, feeling my good mood drop a little.

"It's not that bad, but I just need you to check it out and then tell me if we should replace the entire chandelier or just order a part for it." I sighed heavily but then headed over to the room.

We arrived at the banquet room, and I opened the door to a dark room.

I felt the side of the wall to find the switch and flicked it on.

"SURPRISE!" About 100 voices rang out.

I was a little taken aback, and Chef Stark steadied me from falling back.

"It's all for you, Nikki." He said with a large smile.

Everyone was here: Matt, Sara, Jagger, Mrs.Green, Jessica and her beau, Roxy, Paul, Marge, Betty Jean, Craig, Kiana, Martin, Oliver, Daisy, Mayor CJ, Lisa, my new employee, my band gals, and many others.

The music played a tune of Happy Birthday, and then one of my waiters rolled out a beautiful three-tiered cake in pale yellow with flowers on top.

The candles on top of the cake were simple, a three and a zero to mark my 30th birthday on the 30th of August.

My golden birthday.

After that the evening was a bit of a whirlwind, we ate, we laughed, and we danced to the music played by the DJ.

I took so many photos with my guests that my smile was hurting by the end of the night. When I finally got home, I collapsed in bed, so glad to be another year older and wiser.

The next day, Paul came by just after I had put some coffee on.

I was going to swing by the mansion to work with the construction team on the upgrades to the electrical and the decorators to go over the paint and window treatments.

"Hi Nikki, I'm sorry to bother you this morning, but I had to tell you in person."

"What's going on Paul?"

Stacie McDaniels was transferred to a mental health hospital for her evaluation, and somehow she escaped! They can't find her."

"Oh my gosh." I was shocked that Stacie was on the run.

Would she be back? Would she find someplace to start over?

What would happen to everyone here?

"I don't want to be looking over my shoulder for the rest of my life. Do you think she would try anything?"

I asked Paul. "I don't think you have to worry about her. I think she's going to stay away from here. I think she's on to a new adventure with new people to sabotage and victimize.

I'm keeping in touch with Caleb, and he has some people on this case, and they have a network all over the US and Europe that can help us.

She's not Jason Bourne; she can't hide for very long."

"Yeah, I guess so, at some point, karma will come for her."

EPILOGUE

Stacie McDaniels walked through the town of Venice, Italy. The sun shone brightly along the bay where the boats lay drifting and bobbing in the water. The people and merchants filled the market with chatter, laughter, and long conversations.

The buying, selling, and negotiating of goods, produce, flowers, and grains went about the usual business. Stacie made her way to her hotel, The Gritti Palace.

A beautiful building, once home to Andrea Gritti, the Doge of Venice, as well as being home to other nobles.

Filled with Terrazzo floors, priceless artwork, and fabulous antiques, and Gothic influences. The place was a masterpiece. Marble and stone baths and iron terraces overlooking the grand canals of Venice. Simply beautiful!

Stacie walked into the hotel and checked into her room overlooking the boats down below. She had the bellhop place her four cases of Louis Vuitton luggage in the bedroom closet of the Pisani Palazzo Canal Suite. She tipped the young man, and he thanked her in English.

"Thank you, signorina." He tipped his hat and smiled.

After he left, she bathed and dressed for dinner in town.

By 7 pm, she was fabulous in a low-cut, strapless, vibrant purple gown in silk.

She pulled a black cashmere wrap from the closet, then she placed her passport and some cash in the hotel safe.

In her small black satin clutch, she took her credit cards, fake ID, and a tube of Yves Saint Laurent lipstick.

She admired herself in the mirror, looking herself up and down with admiration.

"You're a stunning bitch."

She smiled wickedly and tossed her wrap about her bare shoulders.

Greeted by the staff in the lobby and admired by people coming and going and complimenting her appearance, Stacie felt on top again, back in the world as a woman with money and power.

She had vowed never to go back to the States and instead live in Europe and tour many of the countries until she found the right place to settle down in.

She had a Swiss account with 3.5 million dollars in it, and although she knew it wouldn't last forever, so she had a list of the top ten richest men in Europe.

She knew exactly who she was going to entertain, and soon she wouldn't be concerned with money.

In the meantime, before she sought out her prince, she decided to enjoy some time in Italy before venturing to Spain to find the man she wanted to marry.

The waiting gondola on the water was her transportation to take her to one of the most popular restaurants in Venice.

A new bistro with a fun and elegant atmosphere and award-winning food.

She arrived at the Champagne Rosa, or in English, it was called Pink Champagne Restaurant.

She was helped out of the gondola and then walked into the elegant lobby, where she asked for a table in the bar.

She ordered a martini and a fig and cheese green salad.

She perused the room of people, some with dates and some single men. She had her eye on a few of them until the one that she wanted to talk to came up to her table.

"I know this sounds cliche, but I couldn't help but notice you across the bar."

A very handsome man in his early 30s or so said. Perfect English with a slight Italian accent.

His hazel eyes sparkled with flecks of gold in them.

His short black hair neatly gelled resembled a 1950s actor in a Hollywood movie, from a more elegant time.

Dressed in a black Armani suit and expensive Italian shoes, Stacie felt she could give her attention to him.

He joined her at her table, and they struck up a conversation.

He told her of his work as a lawyer in Positano, Italy, and that he was on a short vacation to attend the wedding of a friend.

They dined, drank, and laughed, and after an hour, they decided to leave the restaurant and ride in a gondola around the canals.

They sat side by side in a gondola and slowly sailed around the many buildings. It was dark and now getting a little chilly.

He draped his coat over her, and she snuggled closer to him.

They sailed in a small canal where the buildings were dark and the half-moonlight barely reached them. He began to kiss her passionately.

She wrapped her arms around him. He held her face and moved his hand to the back of her neck, massaging it and wrapping his hand around the back of her head. Kissing her neck, with light kisses that made her melt.

She was lost in passion, in the midnight of the canal and the moment of pure romance that filled her mind.

It was fast! She didn't feel much pain, and in one swift moment, he took her life! A quick snap of her neck, and she was gone.

She slumped over, and he dumped her in the dark water, a drifting beauty in purple. She floated away from the gondola.

The handsome man told the gondolier to take him to the boss's office, and on they sailed until they reached a brick building a few canals to the east.

The man got out of the small gondola and signaled to the gondolier a light wave; they were in the same employment, and they signaled to one another a job well done.

The handsome man walked into the brick building and upstairs to a fine office, stately, decorated, and elegant with tapestries and fine rugs.

A large antique desk with a soft fabric chair in dark red is where the boss sat.

"Boss, I took care of the problem."

The handsome man sat in a chair across from the man in charge.

"Good work." He said smoking a cigar

"It's too bad boss, she was a beautiful woman."

"Yes, Antony, but she was damaged goods and needed to be dealt with! We take care of our friends, family, and those who did right by us; we repay our debts."

"Is there anything else, boss?"

"No, Antony, go home."

"Ok boss."

The handsome man left, and the boss picked up the phone on his desk.

The line rang twice, and then it was answered.

"Tony, it's done! Her body will be found tomorrow. Make sure Nikki finds out."

"I will, Donnie, thank you."

"We take care of our friends, and I'm glad to pay back my debt to Nikki, and now she won't have to worry about this woman coming back to finish what she started."

"That's good news, Donnie."

"Alright, my friend, take care."

"You as well Donnie."

Donnie Giacomo smiled with satisfaction.

He turned off the lights in his office and left for his villa in Tuscany.

A note from the author about the inspiration for the

Rancho Santa Ariana Mansion and Estate.

Book 6 of the Nikki Rodriguez mysteries was inspired by so many

different historic homes and estates, but one that I envisioned for

this book came from a home located in Arcadia, California.

A city near and dear to me, and part of the San Gabriel Valley,

where I grew up in.

Arcadia was once filled with a community of homes for more

affluent residents and shopping, always known as a fine city, not to

mention it is also the home to many beautiful peacocks.

The peacocks roam around neighboring streets freely from the Los

Angeles County Arboretum & Botanic Garden located nearby.

Arcadia is also home to a large mall, and next to it is the historic

Santa Anita Race Track.

Arcadia has a long history of attracting horse racing enthusiasts

and tourists.

There was always one home that I passed by when my mother

drove me to school, and this one place had a tall wall surrounding

it, but once in a while, the front gates were open, and you could

catch a glimpse of a large old mansion.

The Anoakia Mansion belonged to Anita Baldwin, the daughter of Lucky Baldwin, the famed California real estate investor, horse breeder, and racer. He also built the Queen Anne cottage for his wife that sits on the grounds of the Arboretum, and one you have probably seen on the original Fantasy Island, the white house with red trim.

Lucky is also responsible for building the great city of Arcadia. Anita built the mansion, a 17,000-square-foot residence in an Italian Renaissance revival style, on the 19-acre estate.

It boasted 50 rooms, a Parthenon bath house and gymnasium, and a large pool, along with horse stables, tennis courts, pergolas, and preserved oak woodlands.

When she died in 1939, the property and the home went through different hands, it became a private school from 1967 to 1990 The school owned the property and wanted to keep the estate intact and add new homes around it.

By 1999, new ownership of the mansion and estate, along with the city, agreed and voted to demolish the mansion, even after many community members fought to keep the mansion intact.

The home was demolished in 2000 to make room for 31 luxury home sites.

Some elements of the home were salvaged, and only the front gatehouse was rebuilt and saved as a security check-in.

A home in Anoakia Estates will cost you anywhere from $ 4.1 million to $ 6 million, with association dues at $680 a month, with 24-hour security in a gated community.

We should strive to preserve our historical sites and allow future generations to appreciate what the past has given us.

Don't miss the next exciting adventure in the Nikki Rodriguez

Mystery Series #7

Cowboys, Counterfeit, and *Country Music*

The county fair has arrived in Rancho Niguel, and everyone has gone country western for an end-of-the-summer extravaganza.

It's more than rodeos, farm animals, burgers, dogs, funnel cakes, and famous potato salad, it's murder!

Nikki and her friends from the investigation club get together to try and catch a ring of counterfeiters when Jessica becomes the latest victim.

While Paul and Craig are hot on a murder suspect tied to the fair, the much-anticipated policeman's BBQ comes around, and both men declare their love for Nikki.

Will Nikki finally choose between the two men she loves? Will there be heartbreak or harmony with a glass of sweet tea?

The cowboy boots are on, Nikki's friends have chosen sides, and Team Paul and Team Matt are ready for tug-of-war.

Can Nikki make her friends happy, choose a suitor, and catch a killer on horseback, or will she get bucked off and line dance to her death?